Unfaithful 2: Nicole's Revenge

By Billie Dureyea Shell

Published by:
L.O. Quent Publishing House
Los Angeles, CA
Email: unfaithfultrilogy@gmail.com

Cover Design : Kenny Writes
ISBN:978-06921579-1-6
10987654321

This book is dedicated to

My beautiful wife Shatoya Shell, I love you 1437 forever. And also to
my mother Mclessie Shell and all my children. You all are the reason
that I smile.

Acknowledgments

First and foremost I have to give all honor and praise to my Lord and Savior Jesus Christ without him none of this would be possible. Lord, thank you for always having my back and never giving up on me. Thank you for giving me hope when I thought that doing all this was pointless. You are an awesome God and I will never stop giving you the praise and glory you deserve.

Since Unfaithful Part 1 came out, a lot has happened in my life. So many people have come and gone not only trying to grab and dash but also taking pieces of my heart with them. A snake will always show their true self. No matter how hard they try to hide their true face it's in their nature to bite you and they will every time, so if you let a snake in your life don't be mad at anyone but yourself when they do what they do best. You knew what the outcome would be before you started fuck'in with 'em. Y'all know who you are so I don't need to say names but one name I can't go without mentioning April Hadley. I never thought you would be the one to show me that anyone can cross you. But I'm a mongoose and that's why in the end I came out on top (I eat snakes) so keep slithering around trying to get close to me and you'll find yourself being my next meal.

Now to my real family and friends, Mom more than words can ever express I love you we have been through some hard times together and when I need you, you have my back, we may not always see eye to eye and at times it may seem like I'm not listening to your advice but I want you to know that I'm always listening to you alway'z.... I don't know where I would be if it wasn't for some of the things you've taught me and advice you've given me over the years. You only get one mother and I am glad I got you.

To all my sisters and brothers I love you all, there's a lot we need to catch up on so much time missed but there's so much time left let's make the best of it get at your brother. To my children Jazmine T. Shell, Ant Juan Shell,

Acknowledgments

Dureyea Billie, Alura Shell, David Neal, Dillon Neal, Diavion Shell, Preniece Shell, Shaniece Shell, Anthony Hatley, and Cam-Cam all of you are my heart beat you are the reason I am still able to smile each one of you have made me a better person and I am proud of you. I love you with all my heart and soul and all that I do is for you.

Jazmine know that I am so, so proud of you for staying in school and going to college after you had my grandson. You are the true definition of a young woman with a goal. Jordan my grandson I love you be good and listen to your mom she is a very smart young woman and she always has been.

To my little sister Glenda you already know I love you blackie we been through a lot growing up but we always had each other I got your back sis no matter what!

To my beautiful wife Shatoya Shanay Shell there isn't enough words in the English language for me to express how much I love you and how much you mean to me you are my world I never thought I would find someone that truly completed me until I met you bring me more joy then I ever could of imagined. Even when you get on my last nerve I can't picture my life without you. You are the blessing that I've been asking God for all my life and it's because of you that I now believe that angels walk here on earth because your one of them 1 4 3 7 for always and forever. Our family mean the world to me and I wouldn't change a thing.

Janice Washinton I love you so much Zanna and Zalen Addison I love y'all and miss you so much Tara I love you Uncle Woody I miss you more than you will ever know auntie Ollie love you my nigga Jamal I love you Auntie Sadie I love you Cousin Ty Addison I love you Auntie Chris I love you

My nephew Lil Brain I love you stay strong to all my real Compton niggas Yaah! Y'all know what time it is 700 blocc bullys! To those of you that I didn't mention some of you I might have forgotten others of you I don't give a fuck about I wouldn't 't piss in your mouth if you were stranded in a dessert and dying of thirst. To my boy that typed this up for me Kevin Cabrera Thank you, you were a great help. To Dr. Rosie I love you, thank you for believing in me. To all the haters keep hating y'all make me better. As long as you keep hating I must be doing something right. When you stop hating that is when I will start worrying.

To all my fans thank you for reading I hope you enjoy

Acknowledgments

Nicole's Revenge as much as I enjoyed writing it. I will look forward to your feedback and just know when you are enjoying part 2 I am already working on part 3. So hit me with those reviews and with that I'm out.

Unfaithful 2: Nicole's Revenge

By Billie Dureyea Shell

Prologue

God, protect me from my family and friends, I can handle my enemies. Never let the ones I love hurt me to the point of hatred, because at that point I don't know if I would be able to give what they done to me, to you and not deal with it myself. (Amen)

Nicole never forgot that her grandmother would alway'z say this at the start of her prayers. At the time Nicole was too young and didn't understand or believe what her granny was saying applied to her, at the time her only friend was Tasha and Tasha was like her sister, "so why ask god to protect her from Tasha?" Now 15 years after her grandmothers death,

Nicole clearly understood what her granny meant as she woke up at the hospital pregnant, shot and with the person she considered being like her own flesh and blood staring down at her smiling, just as pregnant as she was and by her man. Nicole rolled her eyes,

"This bitch ain't the anointed sister I never had," Nicole though to herself.

"She's one of my worst enemies, but the cold part is this bitch doesn't even know I know that she was giving my nigga an ultimatum on leaving me for her. This diabolical bitch got me fucked up, but I'ma play her ass and pay her back for betraying me and fucking my nigga. On top of all that she got pregnant. Ooow you snake bitch I got something fo yo slick ass!" Nicole faked a smile as her thoughts still ran wile.

"Hey sis!" Nicole said wanting to wrap her IV cord around Tasha's neck and choke her to death.

"Hey yourself , how are you doing?" Tasha asked now grabbing Nicole's hand. Nicole wanted to snatch her hand back, it felt like the devil himself, had touched her. Nicole held her composure

"I'm okay, hanging in there for the baby!" One of Nicole's nurses walked in cutting their conversation short.

"Ms. White needs to take her shower now, can you come back later?"

"Sure!" Tasha replied then hugged Nicole

"I'll come and see you again Saturday, I love you!" Nicole half-heartedly hugged her back.

"Yeah, okay I'll see you then." Tasha walked out the room with Nicole's eyes glued to her back with a frown on her face. Nicole's nurse walked next to her bed

"I can see its some hatred in your heart for your friend!" Nurse Kelly stated, which snapped Nicole out of her trance.

"Ooh, I'm sorry I was lost in thought. No I don't hate her." Nurse Kelly smiled warmly and said,

"it's your story, but here is a little advice from an older woman who has been around the block a few times don't let hate overtake your heart because once it does, you become a different person and lose who you really are, plus your baby might come out looking just like the person you hate or dislike, just let go and give it to god!"

Nicole smiled

"Thank you so much, I wouldn't want that to happen!" Nicole replied but in her mind her thoughts about Tasha was that she was the one that needed to be praying because only god was going to save her from what was in store for her shady ass. Nicole got in the shower, as she got in; the nurse told her that the doctor had cleared her to be discharged tomorrow. A smile came across Nicole's face that sent a chill down Nurse Kelly's spine. Nurse Kelly left out the bathroom headed back to her desk saying a silent prayer for Nicole and whoever it was that had pissed her off, because Nurse Kelly knew that Nicole wouldn't stop till she had gotten her revenge . ...

Chapter 1

It had been five days since Billie had been released from the hospital and into Monica's care. Monica had gone out of her way to make Billie comfortable. She had even went as far as going to his and Nicole's house and retrieved his 72 inch 3D HD flat screen TV that was in his game room not forgetting his headset and PS3 with all his games. Monica had also got all his clothes, colognes and every pair of shoes he owned which filled up the trunk of his Jag, the backseat and the passenger seat. Monica had to make three trips to get all of his things to her house which she didn't mind one bit because she wanted Billie to be happy and was willing to do whatever it took to make that happen. As Monica stood in her kitchen pouring a cup of freshly squeezed orange juice that she had made just for Billie, she smiled as she began talking to herself.

"I got my man and I'ma make sure I keep him!" Monica took a roll of Ritz crackers out of the cabinet after pouring the juice then sat both the cup of juice and roll of crackers on the bed tray with the homemade chicken soup she'd also made for Billie with tender loving care. Monica headed to the bedroom with the bed tray in her hand. She entered the room and Billie smiled, and then lowered the volume down on the television. Monica walked up to the bed sat the tray across Billie's lap then sat down next to him and kissed him on the lips.

"Hey daddy, you ready to eat?" She asked as she ran her index finger down his chest.

"Yeah, I'm starving!" Billie replied as Monica began opening the crackers for him.

"You know I want to thank you for saving my life, I really can't find the words to express how much what you did meant to me, nor do I feel I'll be able to repay you but I will do my best to try!" Billie said sincerely.

Monica put a spoonful of soup into his mouth smiling,

"Baby don't worry about trying to repay me, I love you and couldn't have lived with myself if something had happened to you.

The way you can show me you appreciate me is by getting better so you can take care of me and our child. Trust me I got your back as you can clearly see. Just show me that you got mine and that you love me, that's all I ask of you!" Monica said as she fed him another spoon of soup, but this time with a cracker. Billie ate the soup and crackers then looked deep into Monica's eyes,

"I got you Mo and fo' Sho I got our seed, I love you!" A tear fell from Monica's eye as the words Billie spoke touched her heart

"I love you too!" Monica replied as she kissed his lips, almost knocking the tray over that was across his lap.

"Damn Mo, what are you trying to do, burn me with this hot ass soup?" Billie joked, catching the tray before it flipped over. They shared a laugh.

"Naw Daddy, I would never do anything purposely to hurt you, but best believe I'd hurt a mutha fucka behind you!" Billie took a drink of his orange juice

"Ooh trust me, I know that.

I've seen you in action!" Billie said, recalling the day he was shot and what Monica had did to Nicole. Monica laughed,

"What the fuck ever nigga, I was turned up that day, plus what I look like, knowing I could of did something to help you and sat back and did nothing. I ain't no punk bitch!" Monica started pushing another spoonful of soup toward his mouth

"Now shut up, and eat this soup so you can get better, because I need some of that dick."

Chapter 2

Nicole walked out of Centinela hospital with her arm in a sling and hatred in her heart. She looked up at the sky, smiled then thanked god for sparing her life. Nicole waved down a taxi with her good hand thinking about the last words she heard before she was shot

"Naw bitch I'm keeping it!" Nicole broke out in laughter as she got into the taxi and closed the door. Sade was playing over the speakers in the taxi which made Nicole relax.

"Ma'am where would you like me to take you?" the driver asked as

"This is no ordinary love" played softly. Nicole sat back in her seat and closed her eyes 13567 Caldwell St. Nicole said with a smile on her face.

"That's in the city of Compton!" the driver pulled out the hospital parking lot on to Myrtle Ave. He made a left, once at Hardy Ave and then he made a right. Once at Labrea and Hardy he made a left then drove down to the 105 freeway. Nicole drifted off to sleep as they turned onto the freeway dreaming of nothing but Revenge ....

The taxi pulled up to Tasha's house at 11:45 AM. It was a beautiful Saturday morning and Nicole hoped Tasha would be home and not out shopping for her bastard child. Her hope was now a reality as she noticed Tasha's Lexus in the driveway. Nicole payed the driver, then got out of the car, walking toward Tasha's front door. Tasha had come to the hospital almost every day since Nicole had been shot. In the back of Nicole's mind she vividly recalled how she had come up with a lie, telling Tasha Billie had already left to Cancun Mexico when the home invasion had happened and she was shot. Nicole also told Tasha that the suspect had gotten away and the police didn't have any leads. Tasha didn't ask any questions, she did her best to push all her doubt to the side and focused on just being there for Nicole to comfort her and give her support. Nicole however was plotting and waiting for the chance to expose Tasha for the no good snake bitch she was. Nicole rang the doorbell. Before she could remove her finger from the button the door flew open.

"Bitch I seen you getting out the taxi you look a whole lot better since I last seen you. What's up girl? Why didn't you call me to pick you up?" Tasha said embracing Nicole.

"I wanted to surprise you!" Nicole replied, hugging Tasha back. Nicole's stomach began turning from being so close to someone who was now her enemy.

"Come on in bitch, let's get you comfortable!" Tasha said as she closed the door behind them. Nicole sat down on the sofa in the living room; she looked Tasha up and down frowning as she entered the kitchen.

"I got something for yo snake ass!" Nicole thought as Tasha brought her smart water and a fruit bowl.

"Thank you Tee, this fruit looks really fresh!" Nicole said as she bit into a strawberry.

"It is I just finished cutting it before I saw you getting out the cab." Tasha stated as she headed back into the kitchen.

"I'll be back in a second let me finish these dishes!"

"Go ahead bitch I'ma watch some TV!" Nicole cut the TV on then bit into a pineapple smiling to herself.

"Bitch you don't even know that I know about you fucking my nigga and being pregnant by him. But pay backs a mutha fucka and I'ma pay yo scandalous ass back in a real way, you're going to wish you never crossed me when I'm through with you!" Nicole though to herself as she finished a pineapple slice off.

"I swear that on my life!" She turned on the TV to another 24 and finished her fruit bowl. . . . .

Chapter 3

Tasha stood at the kitchen sink washing the last of her dishes. She was happy to see her best friend out of the hospital, but was having mixed emotions about Nicole's story of what happened the day she was shot. Tasha remembered her last conversation with Billie as she dried a cup then placed it in the cabinet. As she started washing and rinsing the last two plates she thought about how she had seen both their Jag's in the driveway on the news. But later that night when she had went by to check out what had happened only Nicole's car was there. Tasha pushed the thoughts she was having out of her head, knowing that there could have been many reason's Billie's car was no longer there. The airport does car pick-ups for V.I.P. clients and Billie was for sure V.I.P. The police could have taken it in for their investigation or one of Billie's boys could be using it while he was out of town. Tasha grabbed herself a smart water once she had put the last two plates away then headed to the living room. She sat next to Nicole and smiled.

"So how does it feel to be out of that hospital?" Nicole sighed, and then smiled

"Shit damn good, a bitch was starting to get bed sores from laying around too much!" They shared a

laugh.

"So, have you heard from Billie?" Tasha asked, looking at Nicole with worry and concern.

Nicole wanted to slap Tasha with the plate of remaining fruit that sat on her lap, but controlled

herself

"Yeah, I talked to him this morning," she lied

"he will be back in a few days, he was going to fly back when I told him what happened, but I told him to finish up his business and that I was okay. Plus I have you!" Tasha smiled,

"Well that's true you do have me but that doesn't sound like Billie. He normally is so protective of you!" Nicole was doing all she could to control her temper. She wanted to beat Tasha within an inch of her life.

"Yeah but he doesn't know the whole story, I watered it down, as a matter of fact let's go by the house so I can clean up before he comes home!"

Tasha laughed,

"Bitch I got yo back but how long do you think you can hide this from him?" Tasha asked pointing at her arm. Nicole gave a devilish smirk,

"long enough to get my arm out of this sling, so when he comes home I can do what I gotta do and by then trust me it won't matter!" Tasha laughed

"bitch you so nasty!" She said as she got up to put on her shoes so they could go.

"Yeah you know me!" Nicole said eyeing Tasha as if she was a lioness and Tasha was her prey as she walked toward her room. Nicole thought of smacking Tasha in the back of the head she was holding the plate that was on her lap so tight that her knuckles had turned red. Tasha looked over her shoulder about to make a comment to her best friend; the look in Nicole's eyes sent a chill down her spine. Tasha stopped in her tracks and turned around,

"What's wrong with you cola?" Tasha asked feeling a sense of fear.

"Oh bitch nothing, I just felt a sharp pain and I wanted to scream." Nicole lied then smiled.

"Girl I'm glad that's all it was, because from the look in your eyes it seemed as if you wanted to kill somebody!" Nicole laughed,

"Bitch I do, I want to kill the mutha fuckas that shot me and put me in that damn hospital but for now I'm just happy to be alive. Now go get yo shoes so we can get up out here and see how fucked up my house looks!" Tasha headed into her room still feeling uneased. Something wasn't right with Nicole; she just couldn't put her finger on it. Tasha put her shoes on then rubbed her stomach feeling Billie's child growing inside her.

"It's just my guilty conscious eating at me!" Tasha said to herself as she got up off her bed then grabbed her car keys off the dresser and headed out of her bedroom

"Come on bitch let's do this!"

Tasha stated as she entered the living room heading out the front door. Nicole jumped up leaving her now empty plate on the sofa

"Bitch you ain't said nothing but a word they locked the door behind them then got in Tasha's Lexus headed to Ladera Heights ....

Chapter 4

Monica had left Billie sound asleep at home and was on her way to the shooting range for an hour of target practice before her 5:00 pm yoga class. Ever since the incident at Billie's house Monica had stepped her game up and was now going to the shooting range every day for an hour instead of twice a week. She had also started taking Kung-fu, Keydow and yoga. She was good at them all. She had gotten so good at the shooting range that she was now moving the target all the way to the back of the room, which was a 100 yards. She was hitting her mark each time. Monica liked head and chest shots, when she pulled her target in. That's all she'd have. In her kung-fu class she had made it to the top of her class in just a few weeks. Monica was a fast learner and by the 3rd week she was picked to be the person the teacher would show the class offense and defense moves with. Monica had even put their teacher on his back with a move she watched him use on someone else. Monica had decided not to take any chances; she was going to protect herself and her family by all means necessary.

"If that bitch wants my man, she's going to have to fight me for him and if she wants to run back, she can get that!" Monica thought to herself as she got out her car, heading into the LAX shooting range. As she hit her alarm she saw Tasha's Lexus pass by. Monica looked to make sure it was Tasha and noticed Nicole was sitting in the passenger seat. Monica moved quickly to the door trying to avoid being seen.

"Fuck!" Monica said out loud as she realized that she didn't have as much time as she thought she did. She was hoping Billie would be at 100% before Nicole was out the hospital.

"Oh well, it is what it is, if the bitch step to me I'ma serve her ass!" Monica stated to herself as she paid for a 100 round bag of 40 cal shells. She stepped into the shooting room and put on her ear plugs, loaded her brand new 40 cal roger, hung her target and began letting off rounds picturing Nicole as the target as each bullet found its mark. Monica recalled the day Nicole shot Billie. Anger ran through her veins and her adrenaline was pumping as she dropped her clip, reloading so she could let off more stress on her target which had became

Nicole........

Nicole noticed Monica's car as her and Tasha exited the 405 freeway. She watched Monica closely as she got out the car dressed as if she was going to work out, and then saw her duck into the shooting range. Nicole swept the lot looking for Billie's Jag. She noticed Monica looking at Tasha's car before she ducked inside so she acted as if she was lost in her own world focusing straight ahead like she hadn't seen Monica.

"So the bitch hangs out at the shooting range!" Nicole thought to herself as she ran her hand over her arm where she had got shot in. Tasha noticing Nicole rubbing her arm and cut down the music

"Are you in pain?" Tasha asked truly concerned.

"Yeah but I' m okay it comes and go's!" Nicole lied as she made a mental note of the location of the shooting range and the time.

"Well I'ma stop at CVS on the way to your house to get you some pain pills.

"That's sweet, thank you Tee!" Nicole replied still lost in thought.

"Don't trip bitch I got you girl!" Nicole smiled but didn't reply as Tasha cut the music back up. Nicole last thought before Tasha turned into the CVS parking lot was that she needed to step her game up because Monica was on point with hers . . ..

Chapter 5

Billie woke up at 5:40 pm. He sat up grabbing the TV remote turning to the local news. He watched it for 15 minutes then turned to channel 737 which played all the latest hip hop and RandB. Kendrick Lamar "DRANK" was playing as he got his self out the bed bobbing his head as he walked over to the treadmill that Monica had bought for him. It was the newest model and it was able to take you walking or running anywhere in the world. Billie stepped on the machine and chose to walk in China, picking the Great Wall. The treadmill began moving and Billie's burning began. After an hour of walking the Great Wall of China, Billie cut the treadmill off and went into the kitchen. He grabbed a V-8 fusion knocked it down with two swallows then went into the den to work out on his bo-flex. Billie worked his chest and arms for another hour, wiped down his machine then went and took a shower. He put on some boxers and a wife beater then headed to the kitchen. He still walked with a slight limp from the bullet he took in the leg but you could barely notice it. Once in the kitchen Billie took out some turkey ground beef , grabbed a bag of pasta noodles then washed his hands so he could begin cooking.

"Tonight I'm going to surprise Monica with dinner." He said to himself as he cut the stove on. He grabbed a red, yellow and green bell pepper out of the fridge and started chopping them up.

"Tonight I'ma let her know how much she truly means to me and how much I appreciate her saving my life . . . .

Monica was on her way home from her Kung-fu class; tonight she has learned the shadow kick. It had took her only three tries before she had it down packed. As Monica was turning onto the freeway her cell phone began ringing.

She looked at the screen to see who the caller was and answered it on the second ring.

"Is everything okay daddy?" Monica asked concern in her voice. Billie laughed. I'm fine my warrior princess, just calling to check on you.

"I miss you babe!" Monica smiled then adjusted in her seat feeling her pussy get wet.

"Hmmm, I miss you too; I'm on my way home now!"

"Well that's a good thing!" Billie said mixing the turkey ground beef with the noodles

"I'm cooking dinner for you and its almost ready!" Monica took a deep breath then exhaled

"You're what? You shouldn't be up moving around like that, I'm on my way daddy, if you are hungry all you had to do was call me and I would of . . .."

Billie cut her off. "Listen baby, it's okay I'm fine I got this. For the last week I've been getting up after you leave and using the treadmill and bo flex you bought for me. I've had this planned, so get your ass home because tonight it's all about you. I'm at your service and I can't wait to serve you." Monica's pussy began throbbing all the different ways she could be served by Billie. All the nice and naughty ways.

"Emmmmmmm, I see, so you have been playing me huh?" Monica asked seductively.

36

"Naw baby I just wanted to show you how much I love and appreciate you for being there for me now hurry up and get yo ass home because after dinner I got another special treat for you!" Monica licked her lips as she exited the freeway

"okay daddy, I'll be there in 5 minutes." She said lightly running her hand across her pussy.

"I'm here waiting for you!" Billie said in a deep sexy voice.

"I love you Mo!" Monica was so horny that her nipples were trying to break through her bra and shirt.

"Emmmm I love you too daddy, see you in a few!" Monica hung up the phone smiling

"if that bitch wants you back she gonna have to kill me because I'm not letting you go!" She said out loud as she pulled into her driveway, grabbed her purse and damn near broke her neck getting out of the car trying to get to dinner and the special treat that awaited her ....

Nicole and Tasha stepped into the house that Nicole and Billie once shared. It looked like a world wind had hit it. There was stuff thrown everywhere, mostly hangers, shoes, clothes, trash bags and what looked like zip ties. Nicole noticed that all her CD's and DVD's in the living room were missing.

"What the fuck, somebody done stole my mutha fucken shit!" Nicole stated as she walked over to the glass case that held the CD's, DVD's and some of Billie's PS3 games. Nicole opened the glass doors and noticed all of Billie's games was gone too.

"All hell naw, these bitch ass mutha fucka's done did the most!" Tasha not understanding why Nicole was so shocked and surprised that robbers had did what , they do best take shit looked at Nicole with compassion

"well, someone did break in here Cola, you knew they was going to steal something!" Tasha's statement made Nicole remember the lie she had told

"Yeah but my CD's and DVD's how low can you go, Billie is going to flip the fuck out about his games!" Tasha smiled,

"he will understand I'm sure, I think he will be more concerned if you're okay or not, from what I can see it looks like the fools that broke in here just started grabbing what they could because they heard the cops coming!" Nicole looked around noticing that all and almost of the most valuable things in the house were still there.

"You're probably right Tee, come on let's go take a look upstairs . . ..

Once upstairs Nicole instantly knew something was wrong. She stepped in her bedroom and noticed all of Billie's things had been taken from their closet.

"Damn, looks like they were looking through Y'all clothes and shit!" Tasha said seeing clothes everywhere.

"Yeah it seems that way huh?" Nicole replied noticing all Billie's underclothes and shoes were gone too. Nicole closed the closet doors

"well I guess they were looking for a safe." Nicole said but felt her heart drop as she realized what had really happened. Tasha heard the crack in Nicole's voice.

"Are you okay Cola?" Tasha asked with concern in her voice.

"Yeah I'm fine!" Nicole lied as she walked out the bedroom, headed towards Billie's game room. When she entered his game room, the tears she had been controlling flowed down her face freely as she accepted the truth of what had really happened to Billie's things.

"Oooh my God, he's gone!" Nicole said with so much emotion that Tasha ran to her

"Who's Gone?" Tasha said then noticed that the game room was completely empty "oh shit damn!" Tasha stated as she wrapped her arms around Nicole.

"Girl it's okay, we can replace all this shit before Billie gets home, he will never know anything was ever missing!" Nicole wiped her eyes then pulled away from Tasha

"Yeah I guess so huh!" was all she could muster to say, as she walked out the game room tears still falling from her eyes.

As Nicole walked down the stairs Tasha followed Nicole confused. Tasha couldn't understand why it was effecting Nicole so much that things had been taken during a robbery maybe it was because Nicole knew Billie loved his games and PS3 so much, Tasha reasoned with herself as they got to the bottom of the stairs, Nicole turned to face her.

"Look Tee, you go ahead and go home, I'ma sleep here tonight and try to get my thoughts together!" Nicole said then turned back around and opened the front door.

"Are you sure you don't want me to stay here so I can help, cuz you know I got yo back Cola!" Tasha said with concern in her voice.

"Yeah, I'm positive I need some time to myself so I can think, I'll call you later!" Tasha hugged Nicole again,

"Okay, well I love you and will see you later!" Tasha said as she let Nicole go then walked out the door.

"Yeah alright bitch bye!" Nicole said, and then slammed the door in Tasha's face.

"Damn!" Tasha said to herself as she walked to her car in amazement at how Nicole had just treated her.

"My girl is really stressing hard!" Tasha stated as she got in her Lexus, started her car fixed her mirrors, then said a prayer for her best friend before pulling out Nicole's driveway, driving away slowly feeling confused and worried ....

Nicole sat on her sofa full of rage.

"How could he leave me?" Nicole screamed out loud,

"How could he leave us?" She got up then went into the hall closet grabbing Billie's Louis Ville slugger bat and began breaking up the table and chairs in the dining room

"How could he leave me?" Nicole yelled swinging the bat wildly. After completely destroying the dining room table Nicole sat down sweating from head to toe. She looked around at her handy work and began laughing

"Oooh, it's on you selfish, self-centered son of a bitch. It's on you black mutha fucka!"

Nicole got up, dropped the bat, then ran up the stairs so she could change her clothes and take a shower. Nicole took the sling off her arm then moved her arm up and down slowly, opening then closing her hand with each movement. Nicole rotated her shoulder in a circle then made a tight fist.

"I'ma need you!" She said to her left arm as she felt pain, running through her arm because of the movement she had just made.

"We got work to do and being handicap won't get it done!" Nicole sat on her bed then grabbed her phonebook she looked through her contacts, then picked up the house phone. After finding what she was looking for she called a 24 hour house cleaning service to clean up the mess that she had made alone with the mess that whomever came and helped Billie with his stuff. The cleaning service said they would be there within 45 minutes Nicole told them to remove anything that was broken and clean up the house to perfection. Nicole told the person she had talked to, that the keys to the house would be under the doormat with $500 dollars cash for the workers. She gave orders for them to lock up when they were done and keep the change after they had come up with the sum for their work. Nicole hung up then went downstairs, placed the key and money under the front doormat then locked up the house and hopped in her Jag headed for Billie's office. She needed to find out some information and she knew the office was just the place to fin.d it. She turned off of Alvern on to La Cienega smiling to herself

"Soon very soon, Y'all mutha fucka's going to pay for fucking over me!" Nicole cut on her Mackavellie CD and sung along with Tupac's Hail Mary .. ..

Chapter 6

Monica's mind was blown when she stepped in the house. There were candles on both sides of the door which were perfectly spaced so that she could walk in between them. Lavender rose pedals were on the floor guiding her way which made it even more romantic. Monica looked around for Billie, but he was nowhere in sight. Monica closed the front door. She noticed an envelope taped to it with her name on it and under her name in bold letter was (Please Read Me!) Monica opened the envelope.

A tear fell from her eye as she read what Billie had neatly wrote on the beautiful heart shape lavender stationery which said

"Just because I love you" at the top in gold letters, with a teddy bear holding a key and heart. She read Billie's note out loud feeling more tears rolling down her face:

Hey there beautiful, like I told you earlier, today is your day and I want to show you just how much I love and appreciate you, so what I need you to do is follow the candles and rose pedals. You'll find your next treat once at the end (smile) I love you Mo!

Monica folded the letter then placed it back in its envelope. She held it tightly in her hand and close to her heart as she followed the candle lit rose path to the bathroom. Monica stepped into the bathroom and lost her breath, the tub was lined with candles which smelled like kiwi watermelon. The bath tub itself was half filled with bubbles neatly on top calling for someone to enjoy them. Monica noticed a beautiful lavender and gold envelop on the sink which read "Read me!" Monica picked it up opened it and read it with a Kool-Aid smile on her face;

"By now I hope your all mind blown and in love with me, you know sprung, so gone, wiped, ETC, ETC,ETC.

Yeah I know I'm all that but please hold the compliments you can tell me that later but for now I want you to know that without you I'm nothing. Now get yo sexy ass in the tub relax and enjoy your bath. Once you're done and not a minute before look under the sink in the cabinet there is a gift down there for you (Smile) I love you Mo and don't come looking 4 me either!"

Monica's heart skipped a beat, she looked outside the bathroom door to see if she could catch Billie trying to see what her reaction was to all this, but again he was nowhere in sight. Monica exhaled then began taking off her clothes, she got into the tub and noticed that the water was perfect

"How the hell did he do this?" Monica asked herself out loud as she sat back enjoying the scent of the candles and the warmth of the water. Monica smiled to herself when she noticed the lavender terry cloth towel folded with body oil on top of it.

"He really went out of his way for me!" Monica thought to herself as she grabbed the wash cloth and began cleaning her body.

Monica took about 45 minutes to completely bathe herself, once done she grabbed the terry cloth towel dried off , then went under the sink to retrieve her gift. Monica began crying when she grabbed the perfectly wrapped box with a note on top.

"OMG, I love this nigga!" Monica stated as she opened the box and pulled out a lavender silk robe with a panty and bra set to match.

Monica oiled her body then placed on her gift. After she was done putting on the entire set including the robe she read the note:

I know your looking oh so sexy in your gift and I can't wait to see you, now what I need for you to do is walk your beautiful self to the dining room, sit down at the table find the bell that's there just for you, then ring it, as soon as you do I'll be there to serve you

I love you!

Monica smiled

"oh this nigga is off the hook I'm ooh so sprung!" She stated as she walked into the dining room tying her robe up as she walked. Monica was feeling very sexy and the mood candles Billie was burning had her wet and horny. She sat at the table, and then looked around the house for Billie once again. Monica sucked her teeth because once again he was nowhere in sight so she focused on the table and noticed it was tastefully set for two with two dozen lavender roses in a vase sitting in the center of the table with lit candles on both sides of it. Monica called Billie's name but didn't get an answer. She noticed the small bell, then grabbed it and rung it twice. She slowly sat the bell back down then looked over her shoulder and noticed Billie coming down the hallway in an all-white tuxedo with a lavender tie. Monica's pussy got so wet when she seen Billie that she had to adjust herself, she crossed her legs to prevent her juices from running down her legs. It took all her strength and self-control to stay seated and not jump up and rape Billie as soon as she saw how good he looked in his tux.

"How may I serve

you my beautiful queen?" Billie asked once he had made it to her side at the kitchen table as he placed his hands behind his back waiting for her to reply.

"Monica's pussy twitched

"Oh daddy, you look so handsome, you can serve me however you please!"

Billie smiled, "In that case let me start with dinner!" He walked into the kitchen then came back with two plates of pasta with bell pepper turkey ground beef and tomato sauce on top of them. He sat Monica's plate in front of her then poured her a glass of Ace Champagne. After pouring her glass he gave her a kiss on the forehead then went and sad across from her with his plate. Monica was staring at Billie in lust. No one had ever

made her feel this special before. Billie smiled,"Baby eat your food before it gets cold!" Billie stated as he got up and walked back over to her so he could place her napkin on her lap. When he went to place the napkin on Monica's lap Monica grabbed his face and kissed him on the lips slowly and gently caressing his face.

"I love you so much!" Monica said releasing him so he could finish what he was doing.

"I love you too Mo!" Billie replied then walked back to his side of the table "now if you want to get to your desert you need to eat your dinner." Billie said smiling. Monica picked up her fork and didn't put it down until she was done eating............

Nicole made it to the office and used her keys to get in. She went to Billie's desk and turned on his computer. As it booted up she went through the desk looking through files. Nicole hit pay day and shut the computer off no longer needing its help. She pulled the folder out which had Monica Tillis on it and opened it, Nicole wrote down, the address and phone number then placed the folder back where it belonged. She locked up and got in her Jag entering the address in her GPS as she pulled off . . ..

Monica laid on the table with her legs on Billie's shoulders while he sat in a chair eating her pussy. He ran his tongue in and out of her pussy then sucked on her clit. Monica was losing her mind, it had been weeks since she had gotten her pussy ate and she loved every minute of it. Monica arched her head back then placed her hands on top of Billie's head as he handled his business. She began moaning his name loudly as she felt a gut wrenching orgasm about to take over her body. Monica tightened her legs around Billie's shoulders and locked her feet together around the back of his neck as her body began to shake. She screamed his name as her body went into convulsions. Billie stood up then licked his lips. Monica pulled him close to her then kissed him, loving the taste of her own juice as she sucked his bottom lip. Their tongues danced for what seemed like hours as Monica massaged Billie's dick through his tux. Billie picked Monica up off the table and carried her down the hallway toward the bedroom.

"Daddy are you sure you're ready and well enough to be carrying me like this?" Monica asked while softly placing kisses on his neck and face.

"Yeah Mo, I got this. I've been planning this for weeks and worked out on the bo-flex with 40 pounds over your weight. I got this sweetheart, now let me serve you my beautiful black queen!" Billie entered the bedroom then kicked the door closed with his foot. Billie laid Monica on the bed then started taking his clothes off slowly. Once completely undressed he grabbed his rock hard dick and stroked it twice. Monica licked her lips as the pre-cum escaped the head of his dick.

"Yeah, I'm more than ready!" Billie said as he walked to the side of the bed closest to Monica "Let's do this!"………

Chapter 7

Nicole pulled up to the location that she had found in the file at Billie's office. She opened her glove compartment and pulled out her Smith and Wesson 9mm Billie gave her to protect her when he'd bought her the car. Nicole checked the magazine to make sure it was fully loaded, and then she popped it back into place. Nicole stepped out the car, closed the door then walked to the house that matches the address she had found for Monica. She placed the gun in the small of her back and went to the side window peeking into it so she could see if she could see Billie or any of the things that were taken from her home. She quickly ducked down when she saw Monica walk by and into the kitchen singing with a plate in her hand.

"Yeah bitch, I'm about to give you something to sing about!" Nicole stated as she went around to the front door so she could check if it was unlocked. She slowly turned the knob and got upset when the door didn't open.

Nicole knew Billie was in the bedroom lying in bed naked and that made her blood boil.

"This bitch is walking around singing trying to be me. I got something for you and your bastard child!" Nicole crept around to the backdoor then checked it, it was locked as well. She sucked her teeth out of frustration then noticed she was standing on a welcome mat.

"What are the chances?" she asked herself as she stepped off of it, bent over and lifted it up. She smiled to herself as she picked up the silver key that was hidden underneath it. Nicole stuck it in the lock and unlocked the door then slid inside the back door closing it behind herself quietly and noticed Monica bent over in the frig, with a pink silk robe on and what seemed to be a nit-tee underneath it. Nicole pulled her gun from the small of her back and pointed it at Monica's back.

"Bitch you will never be me!" Nicole said between clenched teeth then clocked her gun. Candice turned around slowly.

"Who the fuck are you and why are you in my house?" Candice asked with a 7up in her hand. Nicole stood there in shock and speechless. The lady standing in front of her wasn't Monica it was her mother but looked more like her twin. Just a little older. Candice took a sip of her soda, not concerned with the gun that Nicole was pointing at her.

" It doesn't matter who the fuck I'm," Nicole stated once she got her thoughts back in order.

"Where the fuck is your tramp ass daughter?" Nicole asked still unable to believe how much mother and daughter resembled each other. Candice took another sip of her 7up then laughed

"Bitch, do you really think I would tell you where my baby is at? You broke into my house with a gun and think I'ma tell you what you wanna know because you're pointing it at me! Sweetie you ain't pumping no fear in my heart so you can take that gun and shove it up yo ass cuz I ain't telling you shit!" Nicole cocked her head to one side.

"Bitch you must think I'm playing with you huh?" Nicole walked over to Monica's mom then slapped the soda out of her hand.

"I asked you a question I expect a mutha fucken answer. Bitch where the fuck is your daughter and my man at?" Candice laughed

"Oh, I see, you are the one who wasn't taking care of home and lost her man. Well sweetheart I don't have any information for you, but I do have some advice. You need to get yo ass up out my mutha fucken house before you piss me off. You lost your man because of your lack of handling your business. Now get out of my house before you lose your life!" Nicole laughed, "you're a head strong old bitch, but you might want to remember I have the. . . .." Candice kicked the gun out of Nicole's hand while she was still talking which made Nicole cut her sentence short. Nicole in shock went to reach for her gun and was hit in the jaw with a right hook which put her on her ass. Candice kicked Nicole in her stomach then stood over her.

"Bitch I told you to get out my house, now I'ma drag you out this mutha fucka, like the trash you are." Candice went to grab Nicole and was met with a gun to her chest.

"Bitch fuck you and your house!" Nicole said then released two shots into Monica's mom's chest. Candice flew back into the kitchen counter. Candice placed her hand over her wound and laughed "no matter what you do to me, you will never get your man back and now your stupid ass will be in jail for murder!" Nicole stood up, and then walked over to Monica's mom.

"Naw bitch because this time I' ma make sure I clean up my backyard I'll see you in hell." Nicole fired one shot into Candice's head then sat her gun on the kitchen counter. She couldn't explain what had come over her but she felt empowered. Nicole pulled Monica's mom away from the cabinet and looked underneath it, she found some bleach and gloves. She put the gloves on grabbed a towel and started wiping down and cleaning everything she had touched including the door knobs. After she was done cleaning Nicole picked up the three shells then placed them in her pocket. Nicole went through the house and started destroying things as she passed them by. She broke a few lamps and even went through the bedrooms moving things and throwing shit around so it looked like someone had robbed the place and it went bad because some one was home. Nicole grabbed a pillow case and stuffed it with a few valuables so that it would look like a legit robbery then headed back to the kitchen. On her way she noticed a phonebook next to the phone in the hallway. Nicole grabbed it put it in her pocket then retrieved her gun. She grabbed her gun threw the pillowcase over her shoulder and walked out the front door. It was **11**:00 pm when Nicole got in her car and drove off. No one had seen or noticed her come or go. Nicole smiled as she got on the freeway putting the phone book on her lap so she could look through it.

"I'ma get the bitch that shot me no matter what it takes!" Nicole opened the phonebook and found Monica's name and number on the second page. Nicole dialed the number into her phone and then pressed send..... ....

Chapter 8

Tasha was sitting on her living room sofa lost in thought. She couldn't understand nor figure out what was with Nicole and why she was acting funny. Tasha picked up her cell phone and tried to call her best friend. Nicole's phone rung 6 times before going to voicemail. Tasha took a deep breath exhaled then sat her phone next to her on the arm rest of the sofa. She grabbed the remote and cut on her 42 inch flat screen TV. Channel 5 news was on as she was about to change the channel she heard a name that sounded familiar to her so she paused giving the TV her full attention

"Tonight in Carson, a woman by the name of Candice Harris was found dead in her home. Homicide detectives say it looked like a home invasion gone bad. At this time there are no witnesses or leads. If you have any information on this matter please contact the Carson Sheriff department at (310) 332-2138" as Tasha sat there in shock she remembered the name of the victim

"That's Billie's secretary's mom." Tasha said to herself thinking back as she remembered the Bar-B-Que Billie had when he opened his new location for his plumbing business on La Brea and that's when she had met Monica and her mom. Tasha tried to call Nicole again to confirm her thoughts and let her know what happened, once again Nicole's voicemail picked up again, Tasha decided to leave a voicemail message so Nicole would get back at her sooner;

"Hay Cola this is Tee, I just heard some shit on the channel 5 news that got my head spinning. I want to share it with you so give yo girl a call when you get this. I love you and hope you're feeling better!"

Tasha pressed pound then 2 so that the message could be marked urgent then hung up. She looked through her contact, found the number she was looking for then hit send. Billie's phone went straight to voicemail. Tasha slammed her phone down then cut the TV off. She rubbed her stomach as she got up off the sofa heading to her bedroom, your daddy needs to hurry up and get his ass back home because shit is getting crazy out here." Tasha went into her room then got in her bed, she cut off her night stand light, and laid on her back in the dark trying to fall asleep with her mind racing 90 going north . ...

Chapter 9

Billie and Monica were in the 69 position when the house phone began to ring; neither of them let the ringer of the phone distract them. As Monica's body went into an uncontrollable shake, she took Billie's dick out her mouth and started yelling his name as she came. Billie gave Monica's clit one more lick before coming from in between her leg then turning from the 69 position so he could lay next to her. Monica caught her breath then began kissing Billie on his chest then slowly running her tongue down his stomach. Once she got to his dick Monica ran her tongue around the head as she stroked the shaft. She removed her hand from Billie's dick and slowly deep throated all 10 inches of his dick. Billie moaned loudly as Monica took all of him into her mouth. Just as Monica was starting to bob her head enjoying the taste of Billie's dick and how he was calling her name while massaging her neck her cellphone began ringing. Monica ignored her cell phone, she took Billie dick out her mouth slowly running her tongue up and down the shaft and began sucking his balls one at a time. Just as she was about to place Billie's dick back in her mouth, her house phone started ringing. Sucked her teeth, then kissed the head of Billie's dick then reached for the cordless phone

"I'll be back to you in a second." Monica said seductively, and then answered the phone with an attitude because she had been disturbed from her duties.

"HELLO!" there was silence on the other end of the phone just as Monica was about to say hello again she heard a voice say

"Your next!" Monica held the phone closer to her ear,

"What did you say? We have a bad connection!" Monica asked not sure if she had heard right. Just as she was about to repeat her question the phone hung up in her face. Monica looked at the receiver frowning then put it back on its base. As Monica began stroking Billie's dick she ran her tongue around the head of his dick as he asked her who was the call from. Monica licked the pre-cum of the head of his dick then looked him in his eyes

"Nobody important just someone playing on the phone!" Monica replied, as she began sucking Billie's dick and massaging his balls finishing the job she had started before she was so rudely disturbed . . ..

Nicole disconnected the line with so much hate in her heart that she couldn't think straight. She almost pasted her exit, lost in thought about getting even with Monica.

"This bitch things this shit is a game!" Nicole thought as she exited on Lakewood Blvd then made a right onto Alondra Blvd. She stopped at Yum-Yum donuts then got out of her Jag and went inside. She ordered a cup of hot cocoa and a glaze donut then sat down and opened the phone book she found at Monica's mom house. As Nicole looked through the book she found Monica's new address on a post it in the middle of the phone book. Nicole smiled to herself then entered it into her phone GPS

"Like I said you hatting ass bitch, yo punk ass is next I swear that on my child's life!" Nicole bit into her donut then looked back at the phone as it showed her how to get to Monica's house from her current location . . ..

Monica was bent over in the doggie style position getting her pussy beat up with her house phone began to ring. It stopped after 6 rings as Billie continued serving her so good that Monica couldn't do anything but dig her ringer nails into the mattress while loudly moaning and screaming his name in between catching her breath. Her body began to go into uncontrollable shakes as she felt herself about to cum. The phone began to ring again as Monica screamed but Billie's name at the top of her lungs as a gut wrenching orgasm took over her. Billie held on her hops still pumping in and out of Monica's pussy trying to reach his own climax. Just as he was cuming himself the house phone began ringing for the 3rd time. As Billie nutted inside Monica his knees buckled. He pulled his dick out of Monica, then laid next to her on the bed trying to catch his breath. Monica snuggled up next to him and began placing soft kisses on his chest just as the both where getting comfortable in each other's arms the phone began to ring again

"Damn, someone is really persistent!" Billie said reaching for the cordless phone and answering it

"Hello!" Billie said sounding tired and sleepy. Billie listened closely to the person on the other end of the phone as he stroked Monica's back lightly.

"Okay sir, we will be right over and thank you for calling." Billie hung up the phone then slowly sat up.

"Daddy what's wrong?" Monica asked seeing the look in Billie's eyes.

"Baby that was the police; we need to go to the police station!" Billie said now wrapping his arms around Monica as if trying to protect her from the world. Monica not fully understanding what was going on returned the affection

"Why?" She asked kissing Billie on his neck then sucking on his ear. Billie took a deep breath then exhaled. He looked Monica in her eyes as a tear fell from one of his

"What's wrong daddy?" Monica asked now worried and concerned.

"Mo, that was a homicide detective your mom was just killed!"

Monica eyes went blank, as she passed out in Billie's arms......

Chapter 10

Nicole pulled up to the address that she had put into her GPS. The lights in the house were on and she couldn't see movement inside the house. Nicole pulled down the street and into a driveway that had a for sale sign in the front yard which was three

houses down from Monica's, and also on the opposite side of the street. Nicole cut her car off and watched the house as she sipped on her hot cocoa a XS sat in the driveway which confirmed that Nicole had the right house. Just as Nicole was getting conformable, she seen Billie and Monica rushing out the house, getting into the *X S* and drive past her driving over the speed limit. Nicole wanted to chase them down and kill them both as she tears flowed down her face from seeing them together. Nicole controlled her anger wiped her face and pulled herself together. I gotta keep my focus; I can't let my emotions get the best of me!" Nicole said to herself as she looked up and down the street making sure it was quiet before getting out of her car. Once she was sure the coast was clear she got out of her car and quickly jogged across the street and to the house she had just seen Billie and Monica leave out of. Nicole walked up to the front door and knocked softly. She looked from left to right then checked the door to see if it was unlocked it wasn't so she stepped off the welcome mat and looked under it.

"Like mother like daughter!" she said as she picked up the mat. Nicole smiled as she stuck the key in the door, unlocked it and walked inside closing the door behind herself. Nicole walked into the living room and noticed Billie's games neatly organized on a stand. A tear fell down Nicole's face as she realized that her man since high school, her child's father the person she loved more than anything in this world had moved on with a bitch that she thought was a friend.

"These bitches done put a black eye in the game!" Nicole said as she wiped her face, and then walked into the bedroom. Nicole damn near threw up seeing Billie's clothes and smelling his scent. She noticed the candles and rose pedals and she damn near went crazy. Seeing more then she was mentally ready for. Nicole started back toward the front door when she noticed more rose pedals on the floor with a candle lite path.

"How did I miss this Nicole said to herself, now following the path to the bathroom Nicole seen a card on the sink, she opened it and read it out loud:

By now I hope your mind blown and in love with me, sprung, etc., etc., etc.

Nicole stopped reading

"All in love with you!" She said out loud as she looked around the bathroom seeing the tub with candles all around it.

"Oh this nigga trying to make a home with this bitch candle lite baths and shit!" Nicole sucked her teeth, then continued reading

"But for now I want you to know that without you I'm nothing!"

Nicole balled the letter up not able to read anymore

"Without her your nothing, nigga I'm the one who was there with you when you had nothing I'm the one who helped you build that plumbing business from the ground up without her your nothing!" Nicole went into an uncontrollable rage. She began destroying the bathroom

"Fuck you Billie how could you!" Nicole yelled as she took the top of the toilet off and slammed it into the medicine cabinet mirror then threw it at the wall making a hole almost big enough to fit a body through . Breathing hard Nicole walked out the bathroom mumbling to herself

"Without you, your nothing!" over and over again. As she was held toward the door she had an idea and smiled.

"Y'all got me fucked up!" Nicole stated as she yanked the stove out and broke the gas holes. Nicole went into the frig grabbed a Hawaiian punch then drunk it, "without her your nothing huh?" She said to herself as she threw her empty can into the living room. Nicole opened the kitchen drawer, found a book of matches, then headed to the front door.

"With her you'll have nothing!" Nicole said as she opened the front door. Once outside Nicole lite the match and threw it back into the house. As Nicole walked away not caring if someone seen her or not the house went up in flames. Nicole crossed the street got in her car and backed out the driveway put her car in drive and drove off listening to Mary **J.** Blige "I'm not gonna cry!" Just as she was turning the comer a loud explosion woke the whole block up light began to come on and people started stepping out their house. Nicole smiled

"And with her you won't have shit, I'ma make sure of that on my child's life!" Nicole pulled onto Lakewood Blvd headed back to her house so she could get her mind together and plan her next move ... .

Chapter 11

Billie and Monica sat in the interview room at the Carson Sheriff Station waiting to be talked too Monica was so gone over the news of her mother being dead that she couldn't stop crying Billie held her close to him as a detective entered the room with a folder and a cup of coffee in his hand.

"Hello how are you two doing tonight?" Detective Jones asked trying to loosen up the tension in the room. Billie answered for the both of them.

"We've been better, my fiancé is taking this hard so can we get to what we are down here for, so I can get her back home!"

"Yes sir, sure, sure, I totally understand and I'm so sorry for your lost. Does your mother have any enemies that you know about MS. Tillis?" Monica wiped her eye's

"No, not that I know of or can think of. My mom, my mom was cool peeps!" Monica began crying again

"I mean she was loved by anyone who met her because she was so down to earth!" Billie pulled Monica close to him as if to shield her from the world. Detective Jones opened the folder well from what we've put together from the scene of the crime which was your moms house it looks like a robbery gone bad there where things broken and thrown around also we can see that

things are missing do you know your mother's house and belongs pretty well?"

"Yes I do, I lived with her most of my life plus when I'm not home I'm at my moms!" That's great I know it's a lot to ask right now but I will need you to go over to her house with me and look around so you can tell me what's all missing." Monica took a deep breath then sigh

"That's fine just let me know when you want to do it

and I'll meet you there!" Well if it's not too much trouble it would be a big help if we could do it tonight or shall I say this morning since it's 1:00 am. Well the case is still fresh well have a better chance at catching the suspect because we will know what we are looking for and will be able to alert the local pawn shop in the area." Monica looked at Billie who gave her a warm smile then nodded

"Okay!" Monica said then stood up,

"let's get this over with, but before I do that I want to see my mother's body." Billie stood up next to Monica helping her put her coat back on detective Jones grabbed the folder then got up

"I was just about to get to that we need you to identify the body so we can get that out the way first.

Detective Jones headed to the door, I'll meet you two at the Inglewood Mortuary ....

Nicole made it home at about **1**:58 am she stepped into her house and could smell the pinesol that the cleaning crew had used. Nicole looking around the house and was extremely pleased with the job the cleaning crew had done. She began roaming her clothes; once her clothes was off she walked to the guess bathroom in her panties and bra. Once in the bathroom she removed her panties and bra cut the shower on then stepped in.

Nicole took a 45 minute shower dried off and wrapped herself in a terry cloth towel. She went into her kitchen, opened her fridge and poured herself a glass of simply social lemonade as she drunk her lemonade Nicole walked over to her purse she had left by the door when she came in and grabbed her cell phone. She checked her voicemail and heard Tasha's urgent message. Nicole smiled to herself then erased the call. She finished off her glass of lemonade placed her glass in the sink then put her phone on the charger.

Nicole sat on her Livingroom sofa then cut on her 92 inch HD 3D TV and turned to the Channel 5 news. Nicole watched listening closely as they talked about both the murder and burning down of Monica's house. Nicole balled up on the sofa with a smile on her face as the news reporter said that there was no witnesses nor leads in the murder and the fire was an accident because the owner had left the stove on and candles burning. Nicole drifted off to sleep with a kool-aide smile on her face feeling good about what she had done and thinking about how good it felt to get revenge her last thought before she was completely in la-la land, was to plan her next move to destroy the lives of everyone that had did everything they could to destroy hers and her child's . ...

Monica and Billie made it to the morgue and had identified the body. Monica damn near lost her mind seeing her mother laying on a metal table with 2 bullet holes in her.

Billie walked Monica back to the car and was putting her in the car when detective Jones walked over to them. Billie closed the passenger door then turned to face the detective. Excuse me Mr. Ward I hate to be the bearer of bad news but I think we need to go by your mother in laws house another day." Billie not seeing this as bad news smiled at detective Jones grateful that the night would be over because he didn't know how much more Monica could take and didn't want the stress to affect their baby.

"That's not bad news at all my wife needs the. . .. The detective cut off Billie,

"Sir I just received a call, your

house was burned down once again I'm sorry!" Billie looked at the detective in shock

"What? You gotta be joking, please tell me your joking!

Detective Jones shook his head, "I wish I was, you two have been through so much already but your house was in a fire, I think you two need to head home, Y'all take as much time as you need and when you get things together you can give me a call." Billie shook the detectives hand then ran around to the driver's side and hopped in the car. He looked at Monica; tears were running down her face

"Daddy what's going on around here? Why is shit going wrong all of a sudden?"

Monica asked. Billie grabbed her hand while he started the car.

"I don't know Mo, but we gonna go home and find out what the fuck is going on, and what or who started this fire Billie pulled off, holding Monica's hand, going 70 mph ....

Billie and Monica made it to their house in about 10 minutes flat it was 2: 10 am when Billie pulled up and parked behind what seemed to be a police car. The fire department was still there (at their home) looking through the debris try to find the cause of the fire. Billie got out of the car then walked over to the passenger side and opened the door for Monica. Together they walked hand and hand up to the fire chief looking at their once beautiful house that was now completely destroyed the fire chief hearing footsteps approaching turned to face them with a warm smile.

"Am I safe to guess this home belongs to the two of you? He asked as he stuck his hand out toward Billie. Billie then said

"Yes!"

"Well I'm Chief Davis, as you can see your house was totally destroyed I'm guessing it was a gas fire because of how fast everything went up in flames. However, we, I can't be sure because there was nothing left behind for me to confirm this but debris. Is there anything you can tell me that might help?" Chief Davis asked looking at both Billie and Monica. Billie placed his arm around Monica,

"well I might of left the stove on because we were in a rush to leave to get to the police station I also forgot to put out some candles I had burning throughout the house. You think that could have done it? Billie asked with Monica holding on to his arm and snuggled closely up under him. Chief Davis rubbed his chin,

"that could of done it no doubt, but like I said earlier it seems like you had a gas leak but if you say you might of left the stove on with candles burning I'll have to rule that as a reason. But as I said before there isn't much left for us to investigate because the house is totaled, I'm sorry to hear about the death in your family, you two have been through a lot I advise you both go get some rest. You can pick up my report tomorrow, that way you can give it to your insurance company!" Billie said thank you and shook the Chief's hand once again. Billie put Monica in the car closed her door then walked to the driver side and got in the car himself. Monica looked at him with hurt filled eye's

"Daddy I'm too tired to think, can we please get a room, I need to get some sleep my head is killing me!" Billie nodded

"Yeah Mo, I got you, he picked up his cell phone calling the Hilton by the LAX airport. The desk clerk answered on the second ring.

"Good morning this is Kelly, how may I help you? The receptionist asked in a cheerful tone

"Hi Kelly, me and my fiancé need a room for a week, we will be checking in, in about 30 to 45 minutes do you have any openings?"

"Why yes sir, we sure do what

kind of room would you like? We have the........ Billie cut her off there's no need for you to tell me the prices or which rooms, you have just give us the best one you have!" Kelly smiling on the other end of the phone,

"Well that won't be a problem at all sir would you like to pay by credit card now?" Kelly asked seductively as she remembered who Billie was and got turned on remembering the time they shared together.

"No Kelly, I have a business account open with you guys already. My name is .. .. Kelly cut him off Billie Ward correct? She asked knowing the answer. Yes that's correct my customer id is 37468!" Kelly looked up the customer I.D he gave her feeling her panties get wet as she thought about how Billie had dicked her down last time he had stayed at her hotel

"Okay Mr. Ward I've found your account and your room is booked, I'll see you in about 30 minutes!" Billie looked over at Monica who was sound asleep. We will see you then and thank you once again Kelly!" Kelly's voice dripping with lust seductively replied

"No thank you Mr. Ward I'm looking forward to seeing you again!" Billie's dick got rock hard remembering fucking Kelly in the conference room after his meeting with some clients from Victorville. Billie disconnected the line then pulled off trying to regain his focus. He kissed Monica on the forehead then cut the heater on so she would remain warm.

"I got you Mo!" Billie said as he got on the 91 freeway heading to the 110 south and I promise I'ma figure out what our next move will be and in this week I'll have you in a new home!" He turned onto the 110 freeway with thoughts of Kelly bent over the table in the conference room looking into his eyes as he hammered away at her pussy . . ..

Chapter 12

Nicole woke up feeling refreshed. She sat up on the sofa still wrapped in the towel she had used earlier that morning when she had took her shower. Nicole stood up dropped the towel that was around her, deciding to walk around naked. Nicole went into her kitchen ready to make her something to eat. Nicole rubbed her stomach

"What does mommies' baby want to eat? She asked running her fingers over her stomach over where she thought her baby was relaxing. Nicole smiled to herself as the thought of eggs, hash browns, bacon, sausage and butter milk biscuits came to her mind.

"Mommy got you!" Nicole said out loud as she took out a skillet, set it on the stove then opened the fridge and took out two eggs, a pack of bacon, a pack of jimmy dean sausage, two hash browns and some Pills Berry dough boy buttermilk biscuits. Nicole reached in the drawer at the bottom of the fridge grabbing a red, yellow and green bell pepper. One stem of green onion and one regular onion Nicole pulled out her chopping block and grabbed a knife. She chopped up the bell peppers, green onion and regular onion. She put a little corn oil in the skillet placed the items she'd chopped up inside the skillet then cut the stove on then waited till they started sizzling before adding the eggs and a little seasoning salt. Nicole cut on the Bose CD player that was in the kitchen and Billie's high school home boy Tony Rodgers AK.A. y.not CD came on Nicole turned to her favorite song

"Make it home" and began moving her hips and singing along to his smooth sound. Nicole's phone rung and she answered it on the 3rd ring.

"What's up bitch, what you doing?" Tasha asked glad that Nicole picked up

"Shit, nothing cooking breakfast, what's up with you?" Hungry as a bear, you cooking and I'm hungry so bitch I'm on my way over there so make an extra plate plus I got some shit I want to get at you about that I seen on the news, I think that girl that works for Billie mom was killed last night, did you hear anything about that?"

"Naw, I ain't heard anything, I went to sleep after you left!" Nicole lied

"But yeah, come on over and put me up on the **B.I.!**"

"Bitch don't trip, I'm on my way, I'll be there in about ten minutes!" Nicole laughed I'm not trippin, you got a key let yo self in!" Nicole disconnected the line then smiled this bitch still don't know that I know that she pregnant by my nigga. Nicole took two more eggs and began cooking them for Tasha

"That's going to work to my advantage she will be the easiest one for me to deal with just as long as I keep her in the blind." Nicole broke the eggs open over the skillet, as they cooked she hit repeat on her Bose CD player so that she could enjoy her favorite song again Nicole began laughing out loud as she scrambled Tasha's eggs wondering where

Billie and Monica had stayed for the night and how Monica was taking the death of her mother ....

Tasha threw on some pink sweats and a white pro-club T-shirt. She sat down on the end of her bed and put on her pink and white air force ones after Tasha tied her shoes, she jumped up off her bed grabbing her car keys off her night stand heading toward the front door. On her way out the door Tasha picked up her Coach wallet. She locked her house up jumped in her Lexus headed toward the 91 freeway. Tasha got on the freeway lost in thought. She switched to the 110 then to the 405 still thinking about all the things that had happened since Billie had went to Cancun. Tasha exited the 405 on Centinela Ave. As the passed the bridge she thought she saw Billie coming out of the I. Hop on the corner with two bags in his hand. Tasha damn near got in an accident trying to make an illegal U-turn. She avoided the accident and was forced to go down to the next light which had just turned red. Tasha not wanting to miss Billie turned on the red light dodging a car that had the right away and headed back toward the I. Hop. As Tasha was driving into the parking lot Billie was pulling out. They made eye contact and Tasha's heart skipped a beat their eyes stayed glued to one another till someone blew their horn wanting to get passed them. Tasha pulled in letting the impatient person pass as Billie backed up and reparked waiting for Tasha to find a parking spot. He wasn't ready to talk to her but he knew that if he had tried to drive off Tasha would of followed him to his hotel and he didn't need for Monica to have any more drama than what she already had on her plate. Billie took a deep breath as he watched Tasha find a parking spot. He exhaled as she got out her car slamming her door walking over to him with an attitude and a frown on her face Billie stepped out the car just as Tasha was walking up on the driver's side.

"What the fuck is up with you? You back in town and you couldn't call me and let me know anything!" Tasha put her hands on her hips waiting for a reply. Billie at a loss for words put his hands up in the air.

"Hold up Tee, let me clear something up with you, I never left to Cancun I've been here in the city since I last saw you!" Billie said sincerely Tasha now confused cocked her head to the side

"Wait, what the fuck you mean you never left don't lie to me nigga Cola told me you was in Cancun and wouldn't be back for a few more days!" Billie now understands that Nicole hadn't told Tasha about what had happened the day he was supposed to leave took a deep breath then exhaled.

"Look Tee shits been crazy, the day I was on my way to Cancun I was shot and......

Tasha cut him off

"What you mean you was shot? Oh my God are you okay?" Tasha asked with concern in her eyes.

"I'm okay now but I can see there's a lot that you don't know and right now isn't the time to explain it. Just give me some time to get something together and I'll call you and let you know everything!" Tasha sucked her teeth, yeah what the fuck ever there's a lot going on down here too, does Cola know your back? Tasha asked rolling her eyes

"No and please don't tell her you seen me, like I said there's a lot we need to talk about and until we do that please don't tell Cola shit and you need to be careful around her as well!" Tasha wrapped her arms around Billie

"Okay I won't say anything I love you and missed you so much it's been so hard without you being around!" Tasha said holding Billie tightly Billie wrapped his arms around Tasha returning the embrace

"I love you too Tee, it's going to be okay, I'll call you in a day or two okay I promise like I said I need you to be careful around Cola I'll explain more to you when I call you!" A tear fell from Tasha's eye, Billie wiped it away then kissed her. Tasha returned the kiss. Billie placed his hands on Tasha's stomach then broke then kiss

"how's the baby?"

"He's fine, missing his daddy!" Tasha answered still holding Billie tightly.

Billie gave Tasha another kiss,

"Tee I gotta go okay I love you and I'll talk to you soon please don't tell Cola you seen me okay?" Tasha said okay then stole another kiss

"You know I got you, but that calling me shit ain't going to cut it you need to come see me in the next 48 hours I deserve to know what the fuck is going on!" Billie smiled, that you do Tee and I'll be there Tasha started toward her car then turned around remembering something Billie had just said to her

"What do you mean be careful around Cola?" Tasha asked looking into Billie's eyes. Billie closed the gap in between him and Tasha helping her to her car Tee now is not the time to talk about this I'll see you within 48 hours okay!" Billie opened her car door helping her in.

"Yeah okay!" Tasha said with attitude as she started her car. Tasha rolled down her window and stole another kiss before she pulled off. Billie stood there watching her leave shaking his head, mad at himself for getting seen. He walked to Monica's *X 5* and got in he started the car and pulled out the I. Hop parking lot head to the Hilton trying to figure out just how much he was going to tell Tasha when they met at her house in the next 48 hours and why Nicole hadn't told her anything at all ....

Chapter 13

Tasha made it to Nicole's house more confused than she had ever been in her life. She pulled into Nicole's driveway and sat in her car for a few minutes trying to get her mind right. Tasha closed her eyes took a deep breath then exhaled she didn't want to go in to Nicole's house looking stressed because Nicole for sure would ask her what's wrong

and the way the baby had Tasha's emotions Tasha knew she might lose her will and get to running her mouth. Tasha opened her eyes.

"What the fuck he mean, it's a lot I won't understand and to be careful around Nicole? She asked herself then slammed her fist on her steering wheel.

"Nigga explain it to me!" Tasha stated as she was getting out of the car

"What the fuck does he mean and what is he keeping from me?" Tasha said as she slammed her car door headed to Nicole's front door still lost in thought. Once at the door Tasha rung the door bell, then realized she had a key she laughed out loud as she pulled her key out her purse

"This nigga got my head all fucked up!" She stated as she put her key in the door and opened it. Once inside the house Tasha noticed Nicole sitting at the dining room table eating breakfast asshole naked. Tasha closed the door then walked over to the table

"What it do bitch?" Tasha said as she pulled out a chair and sat down. I see you're feeling better!" Tasha said looking her friend up and down then un wrapping her plate that was sitting on the table waiting for her.

"A little bit, I just didn't feel like putting any clothes on when I got out the shower and why did you ring the doorbell? Bitch if you was expecting me to open it for you yo ass would have been out there all day because you got a key!" Tasha laughed, "girl I was tripping when I rung the door bell lost in my own world, and don't feel bad about walking around in your birthday suit, ain't nothing wrong with it I do it all the time!" Nicole looked at Tasha chewing a sausage

"bitch you just wait I got something for your double crossing snake ass!" Nicole thought to herself as she forced a smile.

"So what is it you wanted to tell me?" Nicole asked still thinking of what she was going to do to Tasha and her bastard child after she was done with Monica and Billie

"Oh yeah, I seen a special report on this news last night, what's Monica's mom name?" Tasha asked as she put a fork full of eggs in her mouth.

"Shit, I don't know I think it's Candice Harris or something like that, why?" Nicole asked still enjoying her breakfast like she didn't know what Tasha was referring to!

"I knew it, girl on the news last night they said Monica's mom got killed at her home in Carson!"

Nicole looked up at Tasha faking being shocked.

"No way bitch, you're lying!" Nicole started dropping her fork on her plate looking shooken by the news. If this was a movie Nicole would of won an Oscar for her performance.

"I'm serious Cola, I was sitting at home looking for

something to watch after I left your house last night and Channel 5 had breaking news so I watched to see what was up and when I heard the new

and name I thought back to Billie's Bar-B-Que at the office and it hit me who the person was they were talking about!" Nicole shook her head in disbelief

"This is a cold world we live in, that's so fucked up they did that to that girl's mom, it must be something in the water. Ima go get Monica's address from the office so I can send her some flowers!" Tasha shook her head in agreeance with Nicole as she bit into a butter milk biscuit.

"Well when you get her address let me know so I can shoot you some money because I want to send her some flowers too!" Nicole got up from the table taking her plate to the kitchen

"Okay Tee I'll do that!" Nicole replied passing Tasha. Tasha looked at Nicole's ass and she walked by.

"Damn girl your ass is off the chain, let me find out you sneaking around getting booty shots!" Tasha said laughing Bitch please, this shit is all natural no additive or artificial flavor this is 100% pure Nicole!" Tasha laughed, girl yo ass is crazy, whatever you're doing got you filling out Billie going to be loving all that. Have you heard from him?" Tasha asked barely able to keep her mouth closed about seeing Billie at I. Hop.

"Yeah he called this morning, Nicole lied he said he'll be home in 2 or 3 days!" She stated as she washed her plate. Tasha looked toward Nicole. Something in her heart told her that Nicole was lying about Billie calling. Tasha thought about what Billie had said before they departed

"Be careful around Nicole!" Tasha couldn't shake the feeling of being lied to so she tried to fish for more information.

"Did you tell him what happened?" Nicole spend around from the sink

"No I haven't and I told you I don't plan to either, why all the questions? What you thinking about becoming a private investigator?" Nicole asked looking Tasha into her eyes. Tasha laughed

"Bitch please, I'm just concerned, with all this bullshit going on I would feel better if Billie was home!" Tasha stated breaking the eye contact with Nicole, focusing back on her she began eating her food. Nicole walked passed Tasha and out the kitchen headed toward the stairs that lead to her bedroom. Well he will be back home soon and hopefully we can get back in order before he get here I'm about to take a shower and get dressed. You know how to let yourself out when you're done, call me later!" Nicole said as she walked up the stair. Once in her room she slammed her door not waiting for a reply from Tasha. Tasha looked at her food, she forced herself to finish the last of it.

"Something ain't right about this world situation."Tasha said to herself as she got up from the table taking her now empty plate into the kitchen

"On my child's life I'ma find out what the fuck it is!" Tasha said to herself as she washed her plate still thinking about what Billie had said to her about Nicole at I. Hop and wondering to herself did she need to be watching him too . ……. .

Billie got to the Hilton wondering what he was going to do about Nicole and Tasha. He sat in his car for several minutes before getting out and heading toward the entrance to the hotel so he could go to the room he and Monica shared. Billie walked into the hotel lobby. Kelly was still at the front desk working a Kool-Aid smile appeared on Kelly's face as Billie approached the front desk Billie shock his head wondering why he couldn't control his dick as he felt himself getting hard. Seeing the lobby was clear he stopped at the front desk. Ernmmmmm, I knew you couldn't stay away Kelly said seductively licking her lips. Now, I want to know when can I get another taste of that dick Kelly asked leaning over the counter so that their lips were within kissing distance.

"Billie cleared his throat trying to get control of his mind,

"I need to take this food upstairs, I'll try to get at you later, okay?" Billie stated smelling the watermelon jolly rancher Kelly was sucking on

"Yeah you make sure you do that but make sure it's before 1:00 pm because that's when I get off!" Kelly kissed Billie on the lips I'll be waiting and if you don't get at me before I leave I come in tonight at **11**:30 pm!" Kelly stated then stood back up just as a new customer was walking into the hotel. Billie gave Kelly a head nod then headed toward the elevator. On the elevator he got on and pressed **(PH)** for penthouse floor he exited the elevator and pulled his key card out of his pocket. He entered his room and found

Monica laying across the bed watching TV.

"Hey daddy!" Monica said as she cut the TV down.

"I was just starting to worry about you. Monica stated now getting off the bed. Billie sat at the dining room table taking the food out the bag as Monica sat across from him. Billie reached Monica her food and she opened the container Monica poured the syrup on her pancakes and began eating her food.

"Oh God daddy this is so good I'm starving!" Monica said with a mouth full of pancakes. Billie laughed

"I see, you act like you haven't ate in a week." Monica laughed. It's the baby, it's gotta be a boy because I'm eating like I'm a football player!" Billie opened his container of food,

"Well that means I'ma have to find us a big house with an even bigger backyard,

"Billie bit into a sausage what do you think about moving to Himet?" Monica looked up at Billie while still chewing her food.

"Daddy you're all the family I got now, where ever you go I'll follow!" Billie took another bite of sausage glad that Monica was willing to leave Los Angeles because staying with Nicole and Tasha both around wasn't an option nor was leaving Monica now that her mother had died. Billie sat across from Monica in deep thought as he looked at his food he realized not only did he buy more food then he could eat he had also bitten off more than he could chew in the game of life. ....

Chapter 14

After eating breakfast with Billie, Monica decided she wanted to go by her mom's house to go through her things to see if anything was missing. Monica felt it best that she go by herself so that she could get some closure. Billie understand Monica's request told her he would be at the hotel waiting for her to return Monica gave Billie a kiss then headed out the door. 15 minutes later Monica was pulling up at her mother's house. Detective Jones was sitting on the porch waiting for her. Monica parked in her Mothers driveway took a deep breath, exhaled then got out the car. She walked up the few steps shaking Detective Jones hand as he stood to greet her.

"How are you doing Ms. Tills?" Detective Jones asked as Monica pulled her keys out and opened the front door.

"I'm hanging in there for my baby, that's what my mom would want me to do, come in!" Monica said holding the door open. Detective Jones entered the house with a frown on his face.

"I'm sorry about your loss, I'll try to make this as fast as possible. Thank you once again for calling me so soon!" Monica closed the door,

"No thank you for coming out, I want my mother's killer to be found and brought to justice!" Detective Jones shook his head and that's just what I plan to do

"May I take a look around?" He asked waiting for the okay before doing what he came to do.

"Sure!" Monica said as she took off her coat be my guest, I'll let you know if anything's missing!" Monica said headed upstairs to check her mother's room

"You do that, I'll be down here checking to see if there's anything my forensic team missed . ...

30 minutes later Monica and Detective Jones sat in her mother's living room Monica told him all the thing that was missing included the jewelry box and as Detective Jones had thought it was a home invasion gone bad.

"I'm sure the suspect didn't expect your mother was home, from what we can tell your mom put up a fight. Monica gave a half smile

"Yeah mom wouldn't just go out. My dad taught us how to protect ourselves!" Detective Jones stood up to leave.

"Well I'ma go so I can start my report and report the rings, watches and tennis bracelet to all the local pawnshops, you can give me a call anytime and if anything comes up I'll call you!" Monica went to get up, but Detective Jones stopped her. You go ahead and relax I'll let myself out and once again thank you!" Monica feeling the tears began to build up in her eyes said your welcome as the Detective opened the door then stepped out Monica sat on her mom's living room sofa, tears freely running down. her face. As she looked at the picture of her and her mom that hung over the fire place Monica wiped her face then stood up. She grabbed her cell phone out her pocket then called Billie.

"Daddy I'm done with the Detective, I'ma go to the shooting range for a little while so I can relieve some stress and clear my mind. I'll be back to you in a hour!" Billie said okay and for her to take as much time as she needed. Monica disconnected the line after saying I love you and headed for the front door she locked up her mother's house then got in her car headed to her now second home The LAX shoot range . ...

Tasha had finished washing her plate and was now sitting on Nicole sofa lost in thought. Tasha was waiting for Nicole to come back downstairs for about 15 minutes when she received a text from Billie. Tasha damn near scream with joy as she read the text. Tasha yelled up the stairs letting Nicole know that she was leaving and would call her later. Tasha ran out the door closing it behind her. She got in her car headed home. Billie had said in his text that he would come through later on tonight. Tasha needed to get home fast, she had some cleaning up to do before Billie got there, Tasha also wanted to have his favorite dinner cooked for him as well she wanted Billie to be nice and full after their conversation because she had plans on getting some dick and she wasn't going to take no for an answer . ...

Nicole had finished taking her shower and was lotioning her body when she heard Tasha yelling, tell her she was leaving and would call her later. Nicole payed Tasha know mind as she went in her closet grabbing a pair of seven jeans, her white and gray Jordan and a white Gucci T-shirt. Nicole walked down stairs grabbed her keys, locked up her house and walked out to her Jag. She got in her car closed the door. Nicole started her car put it in drive and headed toward Billie's office. She wanted to look up some of Billie's recent Visa and MasterCard transactions on his computer so she could know how to find both him and Monica Nicole turned onto La Cienaga headed toward Fairview with a smile on her face she couldn't wait to get to the office so she could find her victims ....

Nicole made it to the office in less than 10 minutes, once in the office she cut the computer on and began looking up Billie's last Visa and MasterCard transactions. Nicole smiled seeing that just a few hours ago Billie had spent $26 at the I. Hop not even 2 blocks away from their home. Nicole pulled up his business account and within seconds she found the information she was looking for. Billie had rented a room at the LAX Hilton for 3 days for $620.97. Nicole smiled

"You ain't sparing know expenses when it comes to this bitch!" She said out loud as she printed a copy of the transactions then cut the computer off. Picking up the office phone Nicole dialed 411, she got the number to the LAX

Hilton then called the number. A very energetic woman picked up

"Good afternoon this is Tamari at the Hilton how can I make your day wonderful?" Nicole giggled,

"Hi Tamari my names Nicole I'm trying to reach my brother who is staying in your hotel can you help me please?" Tamari with no delay ask for her brother's name

"It's Billie Ward?" Nicole with a smile on her face. Tamari typed on her computer for a few seconds

"Okay, I've found your brother Ms. Ward he is in the penthouse suite room 516. Nicole grabbed a post it writing down the room number "Thank you so much!" Nicole said loving how easy it was to get this information oh it was no problem Ms. Ward is there anything else I can help you with?" Tamari asked.

"No that's it have a nice day!" Nicole hung up jumped up from the deck headed for the back door she locked the office up with a big smile on her face she got in her Jag and turned on her Drake I care CD. Nicole pulled off from the office headed to the LAX Hilton smiling from ear to ear ………

Billie was in his hotel room on the internet looking up houses in the Himet, North Hills and Porter Ranch area. He had found 13 houses he knew Monica would love and was still looking when he received a text massage from Tasha asking him what time was he planning on stopping by. Billie picked up his phone texted her the time he figured he would be able to see her then sat the phone back on the table next to the laptop he continued looking for houses thinking to his self about what he was going to say to Tasha.

"Fuck it!" He said out loud as he seen another house Monica would adore in North Hills it's time to cut all the bull shit and just tell her what really happened and what I'm going to do Billie printed the 14 houses info he'd found then went to take a shower

"Ima let her know what happened, but I'm not going to tell her my plans she and Nicole is too close!"

Billie hopped in the shower not sure if going to see Tasha tonight was such a good idea . ...

Monica was at LAX shooting range unloading round after round into her target.

She was on her second bag of 100 rounds when she remembered the phone call she got on the night of her mother's murder while her and Billie where having sexy

"Your Next!"

Monica said out loud repeating the word she heard as she placed bullets in her now empty magazine. Monica replayed the phone call over and over again in her mind as she slapped the magazine in place and let off all 15 rounds within seconds. Monica reloaded her magazine again and repeated her actions. She pulled in her target after unloading all the shells and noticed the whole face was shot out. Monica replaced the target with a new one put the target back a 100 yards then reloaded her magazine. After reloading the magazine Monica sat it down and began crying while other guns around her went off. She took a deep breath , exhaled pulled herself back together as she wiped her face. Monica picked up her gun grabbed her magazine sliding it into place. She let off all 15 rounds in less than 5 seconds ignoring the no rapid firing sign. Monica reloads her magazine again lost in thought wondering how the call might have been linked to her mother's murder. She popped it into place unloading it once again in seconds.

"Ima find out who that call was from," Monica said to herself reloading her clip

"and if it had something to do with my mom Ima kill who ever mad that call!" Monica finished off the last of her 100 round bag ready to go buy another one.. ....

Chapter 15

Nicole made it to the LAX Hilton with nothing but revenge on her mind. She sat in her Jag for a few minutes trying to figure out just what she wanted to do and how she was going to do it. Nicole got out of her Jag placed her 9mm in her waist band in the small of her back, pulled her shirt over the handle so it couldn't be seen and walked into the Hilton. Nicole moved swiftly to the front desk and pulled out her ID.

"Hi me and my fiancé are staying in room 516 we

purchased the room under out business account, I've misplaced my key can you please help me?" The girl typed in the room number and asked Nicole did she know the customer I D number. Nicole smiled saying the numbers off the top of her head. The clerk typed it in, smiled then handed Nicole a new key card. Thank you so much Nicole said smiling headed for the elevator. No problem Ma'am and thank you for choosing the LAX Hilton. Nicole got on the elevator with a Kool-Aid smile on her face. She pressed PH which stood for penthouse and the elevator doors closed moving her upward towards her destination.

Billie had taken his shower and was starting to get dressed when he heard a knock at the door who is it? Billie asked walking to the door with his towel wrapped around his waist. He opened the door and Kelly pushed him back in

"What the hell you doing Kelly? My fiancé could have been here! Billie asked as Kelly locked the door then latched the security bar.

"I seen her leaving so I know she wasn't here, I haven't been able to think straight since you checked in!" Kelly yanked Billie's towel off him. His dick was standing at attention Kelly smiled

"Emmmm, I see someone's happy to see me" Kelly said

licking her lips at the sight of Billie's dick. Billie tried to focus on make Kelly leave but being a tender dick he couldn't do anything but let his dick think for him. Kelly grabbed Billie's dick and lead him into the bedroom

"Monica could be back at any moment!" Billie moaned as Kelly got on her knees and began sucking his dick. Kelly pulled Billie's dick out her mouth then ran her tongue around the head of it while looking into his eyes

"Don't worry about her right now, let me do me and I promise we won't get caught!" Kelly slid out her dress with one quick motion revealing her perfectly shaped body. She placed Billie's dick back in her mouth and began deep throating it, which caused him to moan loudly. Kelly started bobbing her head up and down making loud slurping noises which was making Billie lose his mind. Billie not able to handle Kelly's head game pulled her up and started hungrily kissing her. He picked her up still kissing her and slowly sat her on his dick. Kelly wrapped her legs around Billie's waist, broke their kiss and moaned his name loudly as his 10 inch dick slowly entered her pussy. Billie placed both of his hands on Kelly's ass cheeks and brung her up and down off his dick which was sending Kelly mind into over drive. Kelly let her head fall back as she screamed Billie's name. Billie began slamming himself in and out of her which made Kelly eyes roll into the back of her head as she felt herself about to have a mind blowing orgasm Kelly screamed Billie's name at the top of her voice as her body began shacking uncontrollably. Billie still hard as a rock laid Kelly on the bed. Kelly tried to evade him when she noticed his dick still hard and the look in his eyes. Billie grabbed her hips.

"Oh no sweetheart, ain't no running, you wanted this!" Billie said as he climbed on top of her running his tongue around her left nipple which made Kelly moan softly.

"Now take this dick!" Billie placed Kelly's legs on his shoulders then grabbed her hops. He began kissing her passionately as he slowly entered her wet tight pussy. Kelly momentary lost her breath as she felt Billie's dick fill her insides. Her pussy clung to his dick like a tightly fitted glove as he pumped in and out of her taking his time enjoying each and every stroke. Kelly began sucking on Billie's chest as his movement speeded up, she tightened the walls of her pussy on his dick which made Billie moan her name loudly. Billie's breathing changed as he felt himself about to nut, Kelly loving the pounding he was giving her pussy moaned loudly and started working her hips in a circle as Billie slammed himself in and out of her like a jack hammer. Kelly bit into Billie's shoulder as he slammed into her one last time releasing his seed deep inside her. Kelly began shaking as she cumed with Billie yelling his name as her thick white cream slowly ran down his dick and balls.

Billie rolled off top of her trying to catch his breath. Kelly feeling freaky slid down his chest placing soft kisses on each spot she passed until she reached his dick. Kelly ran her tongue around the head of his dick then placed it into her mouth which got an animal like sound from Billie. Kelly loving how her own juices tasted, began sucking Billie's dick like a big stick and enjoying it as she did it. ....

Nicole got off the elevator heading toward penthouse suite 516 when she noticed a very attractive woman pushing Billie inside of his room. Nicole's mind began racing as rage and anger took over her. She walked to the door placing her ear to it trying to overhear their conversation. What Nicole heard just added fuel to her already burning fire.

"Oh this nigga fucking on another bitch!" Nicole said out loud as she heard the woman she seen push Billie in the room moaning his name at the top of her voice. A tear fell from her eye as she walked toward the emergency stairs exit, pulling out her 9mm from the small of her back.

"This bitch just made my top 10 things to do list!" Nicole

stated as she entered the stair well, checked her magazine then began peeking out the door towards Billie's room. If I can't have him no one will Nicole stated as tears fell freely from her eyes. She took a deep breath exhaled then wiped her tears away. Hatred filled her heart as she watched Billie's door from the Emergency stairs ....

45 minutes later Kelly stepped out the room Billie and Monica had rented at the Hilton with a Kool-Aid smile on her face feeling like a million bucks. Kelly closed the door behind herself singing Jupiter love by Trey Songz headed toward the elevator. Just as she was pressing the button to call the elevator to the floor she was on, Nicole slid out of the emergency exit and stepped behind her. Nicole pulled her gun from behind her back with her right hand as she tapped Kelly with her left

"Was the dick good?" Nicole asked which caused Kelly to turn toward her.

"Excuse me?" Kelly said just as she noticed Nicole raising the gun to strike her. Kelly opened her mouth to scream but it was cut short as Nicole wacked Kelly upside her head with the butt of the gun. As she fell to the ground Nicole caught her and dragged her into the emergency exit door, closing it behind herself. Nicole slapped Kelly hard as she could which made Kelly wake up,

"Bitch you like fucking other women men huh?" Nicole asked as Kelly was slowly regaining consciousness. Nicole sat on top of her

"Bitch I asked you a question!" Nicole yelled now enraged. Kelly opened her mouth to speak but Nicole grabbed her head and began banging it on the concrete

"Bitch answer me!" Nicole said over and over again as she banged her head harder each time. She asked and didn't get an answer. Nicole snapped out of her hate filled moment and noticed Kelly's eyes wide open staring up at her as blood run out the back of her head. Nicole stood up then kicked Kelly twice

"Stupid Slut!" Nicole stated as she walked out the emergency exit taking one more look at Kelly before the door closed.

"Scandaless bitches get what they got coming to them, yo ho ass won't be fucking with nobody else man!" Nicole stated as she pulled out her 9mm and put one in the chamber as the door shut. With her gun in her right hand Nicole pulled out the key card with her left headed toward room 516 to confront Billie on his shady ways . . . .

Chapter 16

Billie walked out of his room with his head still spinning from his encounter with Kelly. As he got on the elevator he thought he heard a woman yelling "Answer me," as the elevator doors closed. He laughed to his self thinking about what the woman could have been referring to

"Answer me, who's' is it?" Billie said as the elevator went down to the lobby. Billie got off the elevator and walked to the front desk. A beautiful young lady greeted him with a smile

"Good afternoon sir, how are you doing today? My name is Tamari, how can I help you?" Tamari asked as she looked Billie up and down still smiling showing a set of perfectly white teeth.

"Hi Tamari, my names Billie and I'm fine, thanks for asking. I'm in Penthouse 516, I need a taxi so I can go pick up my car can you call one for me please?" Tamari flashed her breath taking smile that won't be a problem Billie are you and your fiancé enjoying yourself here?" Tamari asked as she picked up the phone. Um, yes we are, thanks for asking!" Billie stated wondering how this young lady knew Monica, and Kelly was the clerk that checked them in. Tamari finished on the phone with the cab company then typed Billie's room number into her computer and smiled sure no problem Billie, I had a chance to meet your Fiancé about an hour and a half ago, she is really sweet. She lost her key card so I gave her a new one!" Billie looked at his watch it was almost 4:30, Monica had been gone for more than 3 hours, maybe Monica had lost her key at her moms and stopped by the hotel to get a new one on her way to the shooting range. Billie thankful that Monica didn't come upstairs smiled at Tamari,

"Well thank you for accommodating her I appreciate it

Billie said as he reached in his pocked grabbed his wallet opened it and handed Tamari a $20 dollar bill.

"Oh no problem Billie and thank you for the tip, your taxi will be here in a few minutes and its compliments of the hotel. Billie still lost in thought smiled at Tamari still wondering why Monica came by the hotel but didn't come up.

"Well thank you again Billie said headed for the lobby exit doors to wait for the taxi he came to the conclusion that Monica was try to get her mind right after leaving her moms and just grabbed a new key card and kept it pushing not wanting to burden him with what she was going through. Billie pushed the matter out of his head glad that he didn't get caught with Kelly as the taxi pulled up, he got in the cab giving the driver him and Monica's old address so he could go get his Jag.. ....

Nicole put her key card into the door and opened it slowly pointing her gun in front of her swiping the room with her eyes looking for Billie. She kicked the door closed softly then stepped into the penthouse Livingroom gun leading the way. Nicole walked into the bedroom. Seeing it was clear Nicole checked the bathroom, kitchen and patio

"Billie!" Nicole yelled in rage wondering how she had

missed him leave. Nicole placed her gun back into her waist band at the small of her back as she noticed a note on the table. Nicole picked it up and read it out loud:

No, I went to pick up my Jag and tie up some loss ends, I'll be back a little later. If you get hungry feel free to order whatever you want from room service. I had them bring a menu up while you was out. I love you and will talk to you when I get back. Oh and I found some houses I want you to look at, I think you'll love them, I'll see you later Love, Billie

"Tie up some loss ends huh?" Nicole stated out loud as she looked over the houses Billie had printed out and left on the table with a note. Nicole was enraged at how easy it was for him to start a new family with Monica after all they had been through together

"I swear on my child's life you ain't going to buy this bitch no house with the money that I helped you make!" Nicole stated as she tore the 14 pages of houses up that Billie had printed threw them into the toilets, then flushed them.

"You'll never be happy with this bitch, nigga not as long as I'm living!" Nicole walked out the room closing the door behind herself wondering where Billie was headed to and not able to control her thoughts about taking Monica's and her child's life. Nicole got on the elevator headed to the underground parking lot so she would avoid being seen leaving the hotel still hold the note she'd read tightly in her hands ....

Tasha had made it home and was cleaning her home like it was spring time. She had dusted the sofa fluffed the pillows, vacuumed the living room, wiped down the tables cleaned the kitchen, put the purple silk sheets on her king size bed and lit glade scented candles throughout the house. Tasha sat down for a minute catching her breath as she looked at her guess wrist watch, it was 5:00 pm she had a few hours to get dinner cooked and on the table before Billie was to supposed to show up. Tasha took the chicken out the freezer sat it in the sink then grabbed the greens out the fridge and started cleaning them thinking all the things her and Billie needed to talk about once he got there because she wanted answers and Billie was the only one who could give them to her. ....

Billie had made it to his and Monica's now burned down home. He got out of the taxi feeling responsible for what had happened to their once beautiful home. Billie walked over to the garage which was the only thing still intact because it wasn't connected to the house. He opened the garage and his Jaguar sat there in perfect condition looking as good as it did the day he bought it off the show room floor he smiled as he opened his car door got in then started his car. He closed his door, backed out the garage pressed the close button and drove off, making his mind up as he got on the 105 freeway to put Monica in a better home than the one she's just lost because her and his child on the way deserved it. ....

Monica pulled into the parking lot of the LAX Hilton and parked her BMW X5 and got out. It felt good to have some time to herself to get her thoughts together since all the mysterious events started occurring in her life. The stress was almost unbearable and the gun range dissipated most of it, but the things that kept on passing through her mind is

"Why is all of this shit happening?" This is the type of stuff she read in newspapers and seen on the news. Not in a million years would she ever think her mother would be murdered in cold blood and her house would be burned to the ground. Monica was so lost in thought that she didn't notice nor pay attention to all the law enforcement and emergency units in the parking lot. As she walked into the doors of the hotel the paramedics walked past her pushing a stretcher with a body in a black bag which snapped her out of her thoughts. Panic aroused in Monica instantly, she rushed over to the clerk and asked what had happened praying in her head that it wasn't Billie. Her mind was set at ease as the clerk told her it was one of the hotel employees the clerk went on to tell her that the employee was found dead in the emergency stairway with the back of her head cracked open. Monica shivered at the thought and wondered why all this bad luck was following her and she wanted Billie to comfort her more than every because another person had dead in less than 24 hours. Monica got to the elevator and pushed (PH) for penthouse floor. She watched all the chaos as the elevator doors closed and prayed for the employee's family knowing that this was going to hit them hard.

When she reached her floor she was surprised to see the caution tape on the emergency stairway door her mouth fell open as she realized that the assault occurred on her floor. Monica took a deep breath wondering if Billie was in the room when all this had went down. She took out her key card to room 516 and entered to find it empty. Monica put her purse on the bed, deciding to take a hot bath, soak and relax her mind then after her bath she would call Billie if he wasn't back before she was finish . . . .

Monica finished her bath and Billie still wasn't back yet, she tried to call him but his phone went straight to voice me. Feeling hungry she picked the phone back up deciding to call room service to get a bite since she didn't feel like going back out of the hotel in search for food which all the chaos that was going on. Monica dialed *23 for room service and ordered pickles, ice cream, shrimp, mixed-vegetables, sliced pineapples, and a double cheeseburger with fries and a strawberry shake. As Monica hung up the phone she rubbed her stomach and thought what a crazy choice and variety of foods the baby made her crave. Dressed only in the all-white hotel towel Monica laid down on the bed and grabbed the remote deciding to watch some TV as she waited for her food to come. On every channel she turned to the news was talking about the murder at the LAX Hilton. Frustrated by the events on television and not wanting to think about the woman that she had just seen alive and very vibrant before she left earlier that day, Monica switched to movies on demand flicked through the newest releases and pick Captain Phillip with Tom Hanks. Just as she was getting into the movie there was a knock at the door, she opened the door to see room service with a tray full of food she paid for her food closed the door then helped herself to the fried shrimp and ice cream first, once finished with that she ate the pickles and mixed vegetables with her double cheeseburger and washing it down with her strawberry shake. She was so full she decided that she would save her pineapples for later. Now that her hunger was satisfied Monica sat back on the bed continuing to watch her movie and slowly found herself drifting off to sleep. Within second she was fast to sleep snoring forgetting all about calling Billie again to find out what time he would be back to her. . ...

Chapter 17

Nicole got off the freeway on Cintanela and headed to her house. She was still upset about the note she had read at the hotel that Billie had left for Monica and was not thinking straight as a car cut her off almost causing her to get into an accident. Nicole blew her horn out of frustration as she passed the car that cut her off giving the driver the bird as she made a left on Alvern. Within seconds she was pulling into her driveway. As she shut off her engine she broke down and began crying uncontrollably as all the things

she had done in the pass 48 hours hit her like a tidal wave. Nicole rested her head on the steering wheel, not believing some of the actions she'd taken out of anger, love and a broken heart. Nicole wiped her face with the back of her hand realizing to herself that it was too late for tears and regret. She had murdered 2 people in cold blood and had plans to kill whoever else got in the way of her getting to Billie so they could get some sort of understanding. Nicole laughed out loud

"Understanding, is that what I really want?" She asked herself as she got out her car then went into her house. Just as Nicole was closing her front door she felt a pain in her stomach that brought her to her knees Nicole grabbed her stomach as the pain shot through her body again causing her to lose her breath . Nicole took out her cell phone and dialed 911 praying that her baby was okay, because her child was all she had left to live for. Nicole realized as she explained to the operator what was her emergency how much she hadn't been paying attention to her child or taking her prenatal pills her OBGYN had given her. Nicole sat on the floor in more pain then she'd ever felt in her life hoping the ambulance would hurry up and get to her so she could find out what was causing her this pain ....

Tasha had finish cooking, took a shower and was now patiently waiting for Billie to show up. It was 7:45 and she hadn't heard from him since she'd received his text earlier at Nicole's. Tasha picked up her cell phone and dialed Billie's number; he picked up on the 3rd ring which bought a Kool-Aid smile to her face.

"Hey you, what's up?"

Tasha asked feeling herself get wet.

"Nothing much, look I'm on my way to your house now, I'll be there in like 5 minutes open your garage so I can pull in!" Tasha dropped the phone out of excitement.

"Hello, Hello!" Billie said not hearing a response. Tasha picked the phone up off the floor hand still shaking

"I'm sorry I dropped the phone, I'm going to do it now, you know I got you." Tasha stated as she ran to the garage and hit the button to open it. She walked back in the house as the garage was opening not wanting her neighbors to see her in the see through white nighty she had chosen to wear for this special occasion.

"It's open babe" Tasha said seductively now hurry up

and get yo ass here I been waiting for you all day!" Tasha stated, her panties now so wet she could feel her juices starting to slowly run down her legs.

"Don't trip Tee, Billie said as he turned on Tasha's street I'm pulling into your driveway now!" Tasha disconnected her line as she heard Billie's Jag pulling into her garage and her knees got weak ....

Nicole had been picked up by the ambulance and was now at Centinal hospital in the city of Inglewood The nurse who was in charge of the OBGYN department had set Nicole up with an IV to push fluids back into her system. Nicole was watching BET 106 and Park when her OBGYN stepped in her room with a smile on her face.

"And how have we been doing Ms. White?" Doctor Roberts asked still smiling as she walked over to Nicole's bed.

"I'm okay I guess. I was having a sharp pain in my stomach that's why I am here!" Nicole said as she turned the TV volume down. Doctor Roberts shook her head up and down in agreement.

"Well that's a good reason to come into see me. Let's take a look at your baby!" Doctor Roberts said pointing to the screen with her free hand, and that sound you hear is your baby's heart beat!" Nicole smiled seeing her baby for the first time growing inside of her and hearing its heart beat so strongly.

"So is my baby okay?" Nicole asked with concern in her voice.

"Yes from what I can see, but it seems that you're putting a lot of stress on yourself. You need to stay off your feet so much because as you know you are a high risk pregnancy!" Doctor Roberts cut the ultrasound machine off then cleaned the remaining gel off Nicole's stomach.

"I'm going to see you for a checkup in a week from today. I advise you to take your prenatal pills, get a lot of rest and I can't stress this enough, stay off your feet as much as possible. I don't mean sit around and do nothing because a little exercise is good for both you and the baby. Just don't overdo it because it will harm you and your baby" Doctor Roberts stated with firmness in her tone. Nicole took a deep breath then exhaled. She hadn't realized how much strain she was putting on her body nor did she consider how it was affecting her baby.

"Okay Doctor Roberts!" Nicole said still thinking about the harm she had caused her baby by being careless. I will ease up on my activities Doctor Roberts smiled

"You make sure you do that I'll see you next week!" As Doctor Roberts was heading out the door she turned around on her hills with a smile on her face

"Oh and tell Billie I said hello! He is such a handsome young man you are lucky to have each other!" Nicole looked up as she zipped her black leather jacket. Hearing Billie's name made her blood boil. Nicole was about to verbally abuse Doctor Roberts but quickly realized that she didn't know what was going on in her and Billie's life nor did she mean any harm.

"Okay I'll do that Doctor Roberts!" Nicole responded faking a smile. She finished putting on her shoes and grabbed her purse as Doctor Roberts disappeared into the hallway.

"Billie's the reason I'm all stressed out now!" Nicole said to herself as she walked out of the hospital room.

"I won't be getting much rest until I deal with your daddy!" Nicole said to herself as she rubbed her stomach headed toward the elevator.

"Mommy is going to need you to hang in there okay, because your daddy has to be taught a lesson!" Nicole said mumbling underneath her breath. Nicole pushed the button for the elevator as she was moving her hand away from her stomach getting on the elevator she felt her baby move for the first time. A tear fell from her eye as she wished Billie had been there to share this special moment with her. Nicole stepped on the elevator lost in thought and feeling very emotional as the doors closed. Nicole pulled out her cell phone. She needed away home and knew just who to call to pick her up. As the phone rang Nicole thought of all the ways she was going to repay Billie for not only betraying her but also for betraying their unborn child as well . ...

Tasha and Billie were sitting as the table talking as they ate dinner together.

Tasha listened in shock as Billie told her about how Nicole had shot him and how he had barely got away from Nicole without being killed. He didn't tell Tasha about Monica or how she was the one that saved his life. The story he told her was that he knocked the gun out of Nicole's hand and in the process of them fighting over the gun Nicole got shot. When the police arrived Nicole webbed a lie of someone breaking in their home with a gun and shooting them. Billie feeling guilty for cheating on Nicole and not wanting his self or Nicole to go to jail went along with the story feeling that Nicole's actions were his fault. Tasha's mouth was wide open as Billie gave her the half-truth of what had happened the last day he seen her. Feeling it was best he also left out the fact that Nicole was pregnant

"So Cola knows I'm pregnant?" Tasha asked pushing her plate away from her looking Billie dead in his eyes. Billie still eating, bit into a biscuit.

"She sure does that's why I said be careful around her because with her lying and also being secretive with you about what really happened there's no telling what she has planned or is thinking. I'm for sure staying the fuck away from her right now and I have three bullets in me to justify my reasons why. I'd advise you to do the same but if you don't be on your P's and Q's around her!" Billie said as he wiped his hands on a napkin then drunk his lemonade. After he finished his drink he got up from the table and took his plate and cup into the kitchen, placing them in the sink.

"Cola's pissed off about you being pregnant Tee, that's the reason she shot me!" Tasha got up as Billie was walking out of the kitchen and stood in front of him.

"So what are we going to do?" Tasha asked blocking his way and looking into his eyes. Billie's dick got rock hard as he glanced into Tasha's breath taking hazel eyes

"I don't know Tee, I need some more time to think this shit through!" Billie said as Tasha wrapped her arms around his waist. Billie put his arms around her neck.

"It'll be okay Tee we will figure this out but for now we gotta be on our toes when dealing with Cola because she knows about us fucking around!" Tasha licked her lips let's finish talking about Nicole and her anger issues later!" Tasha said felling Billie's hard dick against her thigh through his pants. She arched her head up

"I missed you!" Tasha said softly as they looked in to each other's eyes and began kissing Tasha removing one of her hands from around his waist and began rubbing Billie's dick through his pants. Billie loving Tasha's touch and taste moaned as their tongues danced. Tasha broke their kiss and gently bit Billie's bottom lip. Tasha grabbed his right hand leading him slowly to her bedroom. Once in the bedroom they began kissing again. As they kissed Tasha unbuttoned and unzipped Billie's pants which made them fall to his ankles. Tasha used her left hand to push his boxers down to meet his pants and grabbed his dick. Tasha began stroking him slowly as Billie's right hand found her clit underneath her nighty. They both moaned with pleasure as their hands went to work on each other. Tasha once again broke their kiss and slowly slid down to her knees taking Billie's 10 inch dick into her mouth. Billie moaned Tasha's name as his eyes rolled in the back of his head feeling her deep throating his dick. Tasha began bobbing her head on Billie's dick making loud slurping sounds which caused Billie to damn near lose his mind. Just as Billie was about to unload his seed into Tasha's mouth Tasha pulled his dick out of her mouth then slowly stood up and pushed him on the bed. Billie shocked and taken off guard by the sudden movement looked up at Tasha curiously as she removed her nighty with a devilish grin on her face revealing her beautiful even toned body. Billie took a deep breath, exhaled then shook his head in amazement not able to believe how he had three of the most beautiful breath taking women in the world in love with him and willing to do whatever it took to please him. Tasha climbed on top of him straddling his dick and slowly let herself down on it. Taking him inside her pussy an inch at a time. Billie grabbed her hips helping her to take all of him inside of her tight wet pussy. Tasha eyes rolled in the back of her head and she moaned as Billie's dick filled her. Tasha placed her hands on Billie's chest and was starting to work her hips in a circle when her cell phone rang. Tasha was so caught up in the pleasure she was feeling she paid her phone no attention. Billie noticing Tasha's nipples hard and calling for some affection began sucking on them as if he was a new born baby. As Tasha Continued slowly working her hips in a snake like motion riding his dick, as if her life depended on it as he phone continued to ring....

Nicole was now standing in the hospital lobby with her phone still in her hand, her call to Tasha had went to voicemail on the 5th ring. Nicole had left an urgent message and was now texting Tasha telling her she needed to be picked up from the hospital.

"This ratchet ass bitch better answer her phone, I ain't got time for all this!" Nicole said out loud finishing the text and deciding to try Tasha's house phone

"Her snake as needs to be thankful I didn't take her scandalous ass out first!" Nicole stated as she pressed send and the phone began to ring as she paced back and forward in the hospital lobby . . ..

Tasha was now bent over in the doggie style position getting dick downed with her head in one of her pillows muffling her moans of pleasure as her house phone began to ring. Tasha looked up at the phone on the dresser still moaning loudly she reached to grab it.

"Oh Billie yes daddy beat this pussy up it yours!" She stated trying to grab the phone off the base Tasha bit her bottom lip as Billie's dick hit her G-Spot.

"Oh fuck daddy right there!" Tasha moaned now with the phone in her hand.

"Nigga this yo pussy!" Billie now sweating up a storm from the work her was putting in moaned out Tasha's name in pleasure as Tasha tightened her walls on his dick and moved her hips in a slow circle. Tasha looked back over her shoulder into Billie's eyes which caused him to want to fuck her even harder.

"Let me answer this!" Tasha said with the phone in her right hand still ringing as she continued moving her hips and ass in a circle motion. Billie took one more hard pump which caused Tasha to lose her breath. 'Bitch Hurry up he stated with all 10 inch of his dick bared deep inside of Tasha's pussy as he held her hips tightly. Tasha exhaled and pressed answer without looking at the caller ID

"I'm your bitch!" Tasha said seductively as she looked into Billie's eyes then said hello into the receiver with irritation in her voice for being interrupted

"Bitch, what it do? I'm stuck at Centanala Hospital, I need a ride home come get me!" Nicole said as she stepped out the front doors of the hospital lobby so she could breathe in some fresh air.

"And why the fuck you not answering your phone Nicole demanded as she looked up and down the street.

Billie not able to control his self began slowly working his dick in and out of Tasha which caused a moan of pure pleasure to escape her lips as she was answering Nicole's questions Tasha bit down on her bottom lip and slowly put her left hand up pleading with Billie to stop as she looked into his eyes with lust shaking her head.

"Yeah I'll come get you, sit tight. I was knocked out sleep that why I missed yo calls but give me a few minutes to throw on some clothes and I'll be on my way!" Tasha said doing all she could to control her sexual desires and the moans that wanted to escape her mouth. Billie with shock on his face that Tasha was talking about leaving began moving in and out of her not caring about her wanting him to wait till she was off the phone she was going to be try to save some ho. Tasha moved the phone away from her mouth and moaned as Billie hit the bottom of her pussy.

"Bitch what's with the moaning in my ear and shit? Wake yo ass up and get here. Nicole said with attitude.

Tasha now working her ass in a circle with her face bared in the pillow with the phone to her ear but the mouth piece turned toward the top of her head, reached back and grabbed Billie's dick just as he was about to ram his self back inside of her. Tasha looked over her shoulder making eye contact with Billie.

"Okay Cola I'm on my way I'll see you in a minute. Tasha said still trying to catch her breath now feeling she had a little control over the situation.

"Tee don't keep me out here waiting 4 long!" Nicole said then disconnected the call. Billie looked at Tasha confusion in his eyes, not wanting to except what he had just heard.

"Did you just say Cola?" He asked with insecurity in his voice.

"Yeah, the one and only, that's why I was trying to get you to stop!" Tasha said as she slid off his dick.

"The bitch is stuck at the hospital and wants me to come get her. Tasha said trying to get up from the bed. Billie grabbed her hips.

"So what, that means we just stop what we doing to cater to her?" Billie asked not giving a fuck about Nicole being stuck because he wanted to finish what he was doing. Tasha smiled daddy, you don't want her to know what I know about her shooting you and what really happen that day so I gotta play my position!" Tasha licked her lips but I guess I can let you finish doing you, plus I was enjoying it!" Tasha stated seductively. Billie slapped her on the ass which made her giggle. That's what the fuck I'm talking about!" he said as he reentered Tasha's pussy from the doggie style position once again which caused her to scream his name out at the top of her lungs as he asked her who pussy was it. ....

Chapter 18

Tasha made it to Myrtle and Hardy at 4:00 pm noticed Nicole pacing up and down the walk way in front of the Centanila Hospital. Tasha blew her horn which caused Nicole to look her way with a frown on her face. Tasha let down her window. Bitch ain't no body trying to holla at yo stankin ass so you can take that frown off your face and come get in the car!"

"Bitch what the fuck every nigga's stay chasing this n-e-way what took you so long?" Nicole asked with attitude as she got in the car, closed the door the put her seat beat on.

"I was getting some rest when you called, I had to take a shower, lotion up then get dressed before I stepped out the car plus on the way here I had to stop for gas!" Nicole sucked her teeth to Tasha's response.

"Bitch whatever yo ass still stank!" Tasha started laughing as she turned onto La Brea

"What the fuck ever, so why you stuck at the hospital, where is your car at?" Tasha asked weaving in and out of traffic.

"It's at home, I was feeling pain in my chest so I called 911 and they sent ambulance, once they got to me they felt I needed to been seen by a doctor so here we are!" Nicole said as she looked through Tasha's CD case. She picked future's newest release then put it into the player hoping Tasha would fall for her lie and not asks anymore questions.

"Well are you okay?" Tasha asked looking over at Nicole with concern, as she waited in the turning lane at La Brea and La Cienega for the light to turn green. Other thoughts began to run through her mind about Nicole shooting Billie and her being pregnant just as Nicole started to speak........

"Yeah, I'm good I'm just not drinking enough water!" Nicole lied then started singing along with future's song I'm just being honest Tasha looked at Nicole with a look on her face that said more than words ever could.

"Yeah, okay Cola!" Tasha said sarcastically as she focused back on the road and turning onto La Cienega. Nicole catching the sarcasm and attitude in Tasha's voice looked over at her.

"What's up, you mad about something Tee? Because I'm sensing attitude!" Nicole said looking in Tasha direction.

"Naw I'm good just concerned, this the second time you've been to the doctor in less than a month. I'm not feeling the fact that you not taking care of yourself. Tasha lied.

"Well I'm good Nicole said as Tasha turned on her street, they looked into each other's eyes as Tasha pull in front of Nicole's house.

"And as far as me taking care of myself I got this!"

Nicole stated as she rolled her eyes.

"Okay Cola, whatever you say here's your destination home sweet home!" Tasha said with a fake smile. Nicole mumbled under her breath repeating Tasha's last 3 words and damn near grabbed Tasha by the neck for her slick comment.

"Now is not the time!" Nicole told herself as she controlled her emotions

"Yeah em hmm, Ooh and thank you for coming to get me, I'll call you later." Nicole said as she got out the car then slammed the door.

"Yeah you do that!" Tasha stated as she pulled off leaving tire marks in front of Nicole's house knowing in her heart that their friendship was taken a turn for the worst and Tasha wasn't sure if she gave a fuck or not. .
....

Nicole got inside her house kicked off her shoes and sat on her sofa. Something wasn't right with Tasha and I knew it but couldn't put her finger on it. Nicole really didn't give a fuck about what she was going through because soon she would be taking care of Tasha's snake ass for crossing her and fucking her man. Nicole grabbed the remote control turned her TV on the flicked through the channels till she got to the news of fox. They were talking about the murder at the LAX Hilton which caught her full attention once the news reporter went through all the theories of the Detectives, then said they had no suspects, leads, fingerprints and that the surveillance camera hadn't been loaded with a tape Nicole got up from the sofa cutting the news off before the news reporter was done giving the world the scoop. Nicole began pulling off her clothes headed for the shower with a smile on her face know she had gotten away Scott free and feeling she was untouchable ......

Billie had left Tasha's more confused than he was when he had got to her house. He knew that he loved Tasha and had loved her since they were in grade school He just never realized how much he had been suppressing his feeling for her.

Billie was now questioning if he had made the right choice of picking Monica over Tasha. Because at this point there was no way he was going to go back to Nicole (after what she did to him.) plus he and Tasha had history together. He smiled to himself thinking back to all the good times they had throughout his life. They clicked and if Billie was completely honest with his self. Tasha understood him more than anyone else.

"All this shit is my fault!" Billie said to his self as he got off the 105 on La Brea, heading to the LAX Hilton.

"I don't know how to fix this shit!" he stated thinking about the shit he'd got his self in as he drove down La Brea. Once at Century he pulled into the CVS parking lot on the corner and parked. Billie sat in the parking lot for several minutes thinking about the situation he had brought on his self. For the first time since all this had happened Billie broke down and cried. He cried for his mother and what his father had sent her through, he cried for not being man enough to tell Tasha how he felt back in grade school, he cried for hurting and cheating on Nicole, he cried for Monica losing her mom and how she was now in the world by herself. Billie put his head on the steering wheel still sobbing as he thought about his 3 children that were on the way and how he had been cheating on Nicole and not protecting his self while doing so. Billie punched the steering wheel as he realized that he wasn't like his father he was worse, he had 3 children coming into the world and instead of figuring out a way he was going to be in all their life he was trying to figure out a way so he wouldn't. Billie wiped his face.

"I gotta fix this no if and's or but's about it!" Billie said to his self as he started his car back up.

"I'm the man and I gotta be a man, I gotta be in all my children life no matter what I gotta do. It's not their faults I couldn't control myself and I'm not going to make them suffer because of my poor choices!" Billie stated as he pulled out of the CVS parking lot he grabbed his phone and held down the 1button as he turned on to Century Blvd head to the LAX Hilton where Monica was patiently waiting 4 him..........

Nicole was just coming out her kitchen with a cup of lemonade when her cell phone began ringing. She looked at her screen, seen Billie's photo and phone number and dropped her lemonade on the floor grabbing the phone with both hands to answer it

"Hello!" Nicole said nervously

"Hay Cola how are you doing?" Billie asked.

"I'm, I'm fine, how have you been?" Nicole asked feeling her heart skip beats

"I'm okay, Cola look we really need to talk, but first I want to apologize for cheating on you, you didn't deserve to be done like that and I'm truly sorry!" Said Billie as he pulled into the LAX Hilton underground parking lot noticing the commotion that was going on in the front of the hotel. Nicole still in shock and taken off guard feelings and emotions that she had been controlling since Billie left her took over, Nicole started crying

"Daddy, I love and miss you so much, how could you do this to us? I would of never did anything to hurt you!" Nicole stated still standing in the middle of her living room where she had dropped the cup of lemonade.

"I know that Cola and that's why I feel so bad for what has happen between us and that's also why we need to talk. I'll meet you at the house tomorrow so we can find some type of common ground, if not for ourselves for our child's!" Nicole wiped her face with her hand.

"Okay daddy that's fine, I'll be here, I love you!" Nicole stated not able to put into words all the things she wanted to say now that Billie was on the phone.

"Cola I love you too, were going to get through this okay, I promise. I gotta go right now, I'll see you tomorrow!" Billie said and before she could reply he disconnected the line, leaving Nicole still standing in the middle of the living room confused, emotional and lost in thought. ....

Chapter 19

Monica heard Billie's voice and flew out of the bedroom of their penthouse suite and into the living room. She smiled from ear to ear seeing his face then ran into his arms. Billie smiling to himself started laughing as he caught her

"Someone missed me huh? Billie asked as he picked Monica off her feet then kissed her.

"Yeah I missed you daddy, like crazy!" Monica replied as she placed kisses all over Billie's face. Once Billie placed her back on her feet Monica grabbed his hand and lead him into the bedroom.

Billie happily followed, watching her ass jiggle which made his dick hard.

"Daddy did you hear what happen here today?" Monica asked as she set him on the bed and began taking off his shoes.

"Know baby I didn't, but I see the commotion outside when I came in what happen?" He asked remembering the crime scene tape by the fire exit as he came into his room. Monica finished taking off his shoes and stood up and started unbuttoning his pants then pulled them off as she answered,

"Remember the girl that checked us in?" Billie shook his head up and down thinking about Kelly

"Well she got killed!"

"What!!" Billie said a little louder than his normal tone which made Monica jump.

"Oh I'm sorry Mo I didn't mean to startle you, that just shocked me!" Monica regained her composure that's okay daddy it's understandable Monica said as she took off his shirt then hung his pant and shirt up in the closet. Monica walked over to the TV then turning it to the news

"It's still on the TV news channels, let me tell you get the whole scoop!"

" Monica stated as she crawled into bed snuggling up next to Billie while he watched the channel 5 evening news in shock.........

Tasha walked into her house after dropping Nicole off wishing she had never left to go get her. Tasha still could smell Billie's scent in her home and was mad at herself for letting him leave when in fact she could of spent the time she wasted picking Nicole up cuddled up next to him.

"Damn I wish I would of never answered that mucha fucken phone!"Tasha stated out loud as she through her purse on the sofa and went into her kitchen to get herself something to drink. She grabbed a smart water out the fridge then walked into her living room an sat next to her purse. Tasha grabbed her remote control cutting on her TV an began flicking threw the channels as she thought about what Billie told her Nicole had done to him and how she had been lying to her about what happened.

"This bitch knows I'm pregnant by Billie!"Tasha stated to herself as she downed the last of her smart water, then sat the empty bottle down on her end table

"That's why she's acting brand new towards me!"Tasha said out loud now understanding why Nicole had an attitude toward her. She stop flicking through the channels seeing the LAX Hilton on the channel 5 news

"Now what the fuck done happened?" Tasha asked herself as she focused on what the news caster was saying, her last thought before seeing that someone else had been murdered was that she couldn't be mad at Nicole for the way she was acting toward her because she had not only betrayed her trust but their friendship as well,

Tasha picked up her purse then pulled out her cell to call Billie to make sure he had made it to his hotel safely...........

Monica was still laying on Billie chest as he watched the 7:00 news when his cell rung. Billie ignored the call still paying close attention to the channel 5 news not missing a single detail. Monica not liking his attention being elsewhere began kissing Billie's chest. Monica ran her tongue down the middle of Billie chest then kissed his belly button while looking up at him. When she didn't get the reaction she expected Monica gently pulled his dick out of the slot in the front of his boxer shorts an ran her tongue around the head of his dick hearing a low moan escape Billie's throat and feeling his hand now on the back her head as his fingers ran through her hair Monica deep throated him and began bobbing her head up and down while she massaged his balls with her right hand.

As Billie moaned her name Monica slowly pulled his dick out of her mouth and ran her tongue down the shaft of his dick. Once at his balls she took her time sucking each one of them gently. Billie loving the sensation he was feeling laid his head back on the pillows forgetting all about the news as his toes curled. Monica now satisfied she had given his balls equal attention ran her tongue back up the shaft of his dick to the head and began deep throating him again. After a few minutes of giving Billie the best blow jobs of her life she slowly pulled his dick out her mouth, ran her tongue up his stomach and once at his lips she kissed him then looked him in his eyes.

"Daddy you ready for some of this pussy?" Monica asked seductively as she placed soft kisses all over his face. Billie now running his hands over Monica's beautiful body kissed her on her lips grabbing her lips as he did so. He gently lifted her up an sat her on his dick which made Monica's eyes roll into the back of her head as a moan of complete and total ecstasy came over her

"Yeah I'm ready!" Billie said in a voice that sent chills down Monica's spine and made her pussy even wetter

"Now let's cut all this small talk, ride this dick like you know I like it!" Billie ordered as Monica's pussy slowly made all ten inches of his dick disappear inside of her. Monica placed her hands on Billie's chest and began working her hips and ass back and forth an in a circle, riding Billie's dick like she was a professional bull rider ....

Nicole was feeling so good from her and Billie's phone conversation about him coming to the house that she had cleaned up the house picked out 7 different outfits, tried on 12 and ordered 6 online. Nicole was picking out one of Billie's favorite pantie an bra sets to wear when her cell phone rang. Nicole looked at the screen noticed it was Tasha and sent the call to voicemail

"This bitch is unbelievable!" Nicole said to herself as she put Billie's favorite purple silk sheets on the bed

"I don't see how she can keep looking me in my face like nothing ever happen and we've been friends all our damn life this disloyal ass bitch!" Nicole sated out loud as her phone began to ring again. Nicole decided right then after seeing it was Tasha again that after her and Billie made up tomorrow Tasha would be the next person to make breaking news. Nicole picked up the phone and touched the screen to answer it

"Hello!" Nicole said with attitude in her voice. Tasha took a deep breath then exhaled,

"Hey Cola, look I'm sorry to disturb you, but we really need to talk, is there any way that we can meet up tomorrow sometime after I get off work because I really have some things to get off my chest so we can clear the air. Nicole taken off guard with Tasha's request sat quietly for a second thinking 'Cola, Cola you still there?" Tasha asked, thinking Nicole had hung up.

"Yeah I'm here!" Nicole answered after she regained her composure

"That's cool, I'll text you after I handle some other things I have planned." Tasha happy to hear Nicole agree to meeting with her smiled

"Okay thank you Cola, I can't wait to see you, with all that's been going on I feel like we've lost touch. I miss you and I didn't like how we parted after I dropped you off!" Nicole sucked her teeth well it is what it is I'll see you tomorrow Tee I gotta go!" Nicole hung up the phone and focused back on getting ready for Billie to come back home and trying to make it where he would never want to leave her are their unborn baby ever again.........

Tasha held the phone in her hand feeling like scum. She loved her best friend and sister and when she was not lying to herself trying to front like she didn't give a fuck she missed Nicole's company. Tasha wanted them to be shopping for her baby, picking out outfits and decorating the baby's room together. A tear fell from Tasha's eye as she realized that she might of lost her sister and best friend over some dick. Tasha laughed arrogantly,

"For some good dick!" she stated out loud as she sat the phone down then went into the kitchen to fix, her something to eat.

"I just hope after we talk we can get through this!" Tasha said to herself as she pulled out some cheese, ground beef, lettuce, green onions and tomato's still lost in thought as she began making herself some tacos . . . .

Billie woke up at 8:00 am the next morning with his visit he was going to have with Nicole on his mind. H looked over at Monica who was till sound asleep Billie kissed her on her forehead then watched her sleep for several minutes as she laid there peacefully. Monica looked like an angel. Billie took a deep breath then exhaled as he got out of the bed, headed for the shower. He grabbed his phone off the night stand sending Nicole a quick text as he walked into the bathroom. Once in the bathroom he sat his phone on the counter removed his boxers which was the only thing he had on then cut the water on. Billie stepped in the shower, he let the water run over his body for several minutes lost in thought before grabbing his loofa and body wash so he could clean his body. He began cleaning his body still thinking about all the things that had transpired in the last 60 days. Billie couldn't believe how his life had went from sugar to shit in such a short time. As Billie finished cleaning his body he thought about Kelly and the last moments of her life that they had spent together. He remembered Kelly leaving his room with a kool aid smile on her face feeling good about taking her some dick.

"Damn I left a few minutes after she did, how didn't I hear her screaming or yelling, she was killed in the stairwell right next to the elevator that I got on when I left!" Billie thought to himself, as he cut the shower off stepped out and grabbed his towel. As he dried off he remember as he got on the elevator hearing someone saying

"Answer me!"

"Could that have been the killer talking to Kelly?" Billie asked himself now lotioning up his body up recalling the anger in the voice of the women asking the questions.

"Damn did I hear Kelly getting killed and didn't even realize it?" Billie asked himself as he walked out the bathroom naked and back into the bedroom still thinking about what he heard as he got on the elevator Billie looked over at Monica making sure she was still asleep as he went to the closet and picked himself out something to wear to his and Nicole's home they once shared. He couldn't shake the feeling as he through on a pair of true religion jeans, a white pro club and his all white air force one's that he might of heard Kelly getting killed. Billie tied up his shoes then went back into the bathroom to grab his phone. Once he retrieved his phone he wrote Monica a quick note letting her know he was going out to handle some business deals. Billie pulled $500 out of his wallet sitting in on the night stand next to the note then walked out of their hotel room headed to meet Nicole ....

Tasha was sitting at home enjoying breakfast lost in thought. She was really missing her and Nicole's friendship and how they had each other's backs an stuck together like glue. Since Nicole had been on sick leave work hadn't been the same for Tasha. It wasn't fun anymore it was now just work. Tasha picked up her phone sending Nicole a quick text:

Hey sis, I miss you so damn much at work, it's just not the same without you =(I mean work is just work without you here and the drive to work is the longest drive I've ever drove without and its only 20 minutes away.

I'm looking forward to our conversation later maybe it's the baby that has my emotions all over the place but regardless I love you sis see you later. Tee.

Tasha sent the text put her plate in the dishwasher grabbed her purse then went out the door headed to work. As she locked her door and got into her car Tasha prayed that she would find the right thing to say once she was with Nicole and not expose to much of what she had found out about Billie and what she knew about what really happened the day Billie was supposed to go to Cancun ....

Chapter 20

Nicole woke up feeling brand new, She was so excited about seeing Billie that she had cleaned up all night fixing things just like she knew he liked them to be. When she finally fell asleep all her dreams where of her and Billie and how they use to make love.

Nicole even thought of all the good times they shared when they were together. She also had a dream of when their child be born, (Christmas day) at 2:00 am. What a wonderful day for a miracle to come into the world, something that Doctor's said would never happen. But God has the last word and the same day God let his son come into the world so would her child's. As Nicole was making herself breakfast smiling from ear to ear listening to Tray Songz fumble your heart on her Bose sound system her cell phone run. Nicole picked it up and noticed it was a text message. An even bigger smile came across her face as she realized it was from Billie. She read it out loud:

Cola good morning I'm on my way 2 C U, I'll be there in about 30 minutes See you then 14 3 6

Nicole looked at the time the message was sent, she damn near lost her mind "Oh shit, that was 10 minutes ago she said out loud as she replied:

Okay daddy, sorry 4 the late response I'll be waiting 14 3 6

Nicole looked at the time and realized she only had 20 minutes before Billie would be there. Nicole quickly grabbed the Bisquick, mixing enough pancake batter to make Billie four and herself two. She opened the fridge taking out two more eggs and another pack of jimmy dean turkey sausages Nicole finished cooking their food and looked at her phone for the time, she had only 8 minutes left. Nicole noticed a new text massage when she opened it she realized it was from Tasha. Feeling like her old self she quickly read it then responded. As red light special by TLC was coming on Nicole sat her phone on the kitchen table and ran up the stairs two at a time headed to the shower.

Nicole striped off her clothes with only 6 minutes left till Billie would be home even with all the things that had happen Nicole new she could get Billie back. In her mind she believed that nothing was more important than family Nicole hopped in the shower an began singing along with TLC as the water run over her body . . ..

Tasha read Nicole's text out loud as she pulled into work with a Kool-Aid smile on her face:

Hey Tee, miss you too, after you get off work maybe we can meet up at Wal-Mart in downtown Long Beach, I gotta do some shopping for the house, would love your company let me know C U Soon Love You Cola

Tasha cut her car off and got out her it still smiling from ear to ear, glad that Nicole had replied to her massage and happy that they would spend some time together like they used to do........ . ....

Monica woke up out a deep sleep an quickly realized that Billie was not lying next to her in bed. She slowly set up, looking around the room trying to see if Billie was in the bathroom or living room. As she was getting out the bed Monica noticed a note with several hundred dollar bills next to it. She smiled to herself thinking of how thoughtful Billie was for taking the time to write her a note and leave her some money before left. Monica picked up the note and read it out loud:

Dear Mo, Good morning beautiful, I had to go handle some business deal. I've put off for way too long. I love you and will be back as soon as I'm done. Here's some money, if you want to go out and shop for you and our child while I'm gone feel free and have fun I love you and be careful, you know you're my life. Love, Daddy

Monica picked up the stack of hundred dollar bills and counted them. Billie had left her a $1000 to go shopping with. Monica sat the money on the bed as she headed to the shower rubbing her stomach.

"If daddy wants us to go shopping and have fun then so be it, plus there's some cute things I want to pick up for you. Monica said talking to her unborn child as she stepped into the bathroom just as she was about to remove her hand from her stomach so she could cut the water on. Monica felt their baby kick for the first time Monica in shock stopped in her tracks smiling from ear to ear well I can see your exciting about going shopping Monica stated now looking at her stomach stroking it lightly you've gotta be a little girl because a boy wouldn't of moved let alone kicked because I'm talking about shopping he would of balled up in a knot, causing me pain so I would have to stay home. The baby kicked again causing Monica to place both her hands on her stomach knowing that her thoughts of the baby being a girl was correct. And your already smart Monica said as she cut the water on and stepped into the warm water.

"Well I guess, I know what kind of clothes to buy for you now. Monica stated as she began rubbing body wash on her body just as she finished her statement her baby kicked again. Monica shook her head in amazement with a smile on her face as she finished washing her body looking forward to telling Billie about their daughters first kicks . . . .

Billie pulled up to the house him and Nicole used to share at 9:30 am as he parked in the driveway his mind was overwhelmed with all the memories they shared together.

Billie remembered when he bought her the house and the Kool-Aid smile on her face as they walked through the house holding hands talking about how they were going to decorate each room. He remembered how him and Nicole made love in every room before their furniture came and how they both had gotten rug burns, then Billie's mind flashed to when she shot him. Billie took a deep breath exhaled he stepped out the car closing the door behind him. He pulled out his house key headed to the front door hoping that he was as ready for this meeting as he thought he was when he called Nicole with the idea.........

As Billie entered the house he notice Nicole was sitting at the dining room table with breakfast set for two. Nicole had on a one piece see through pencil fitting gown with no panties or bra. Nicole had her hair cut like Halle Berry's and could pass for her on any given day. Nicole was glowing because of the baby, when Billie saw her, her beauty took his breath away. Nicole had been paying close attention to her neighborhood street since she got out the shower. She'd been looking out the window, waiting to see Billie hit the corner so she could set the food on the table just before he walked in the house.

Things had worked out just as Nicole had planned and the food was freshly out the oven still smoking as Billie walked in.

"Hey daddy!" Nicole said standing up to greet Billie as he walked in the door. Nicole was looking so eloquent that Billie couldn't control his eyes as they roamed up and down her body. His dick got hard as steel which made him have to adjust his pants. Nicole noticing him fixing his dick smiled devilishly which made her look even more seductive and sexy.

"Damn Cola you look beautiful," Billie said as he walked over to the table and gave her a hug thinking in his mind how much Nicole

looked like Halle Berry. Thank you daddy Nicole said stealing a kiss as they let each other go. Billie sad down still mesmerized by Nicole's beauty and how much her body had changed in just a few months.

"I love your hair cut Cola it fits you!" Billie stated as he pulled his chair up lacing his napkin on his lap.

"I'm glad you like it daddy Nicole said still smiling from ear to ear as she poured Billie a glass of homemade apple juice. Billie looked over his plate, licked his lips the picked up his fork

"Damn I miss your cooking!" He stated as he began cutting up his pancakes.

"Well you don't have to miss it anymore daddy!" Nicole said as she bit a sausage looking into his eyes.

"Because you're more than welcome to come back home!" Billie took a deep breath then exhaled. 'That's what I'm here to talk to you about Cola, I want us to come to an understanding!" Nicole smiled 'What understanding do we need to come to daddy? Come back home, I miss you, I forgive you and I'm sorry for what I did. I was hurt that you cheated on me with Tasha. I mean, it really fucked me up in my head when I called her phone and heard Y'all conversation the day you were supposed to leave to Cancun. Tasha was giving you an ultimatum on leaving me and it hurt me to my very core. I lost my mind, I wasn't thinking straight and I couldn't stand the thought of you choosing her over me. Plus I had just found out I was going to have our baby. All our prayers had finally been answered and our dream had come true and the very day I was going to tell you this I hear my best friend since 2 years old telling you to leave me or else. I was totally devastated my mind went blank and I completely lost it daddy, I love you with all my heart, body, mind and soul, the thought of losing you made me snap!" Nicole looked down at her hands as a tear fell from her eye. Billie grabbed his napkin off his lap stud up and quickly walked over to Nicole wiping her tears away.

"Don't cry Cola, I didn't know you heard me and Tasha's conversation, I'm so sorry I hurt you like that!" Billie said now wrapping his arms around her. Nicole not able to control her pent up emotions any longer broke down into an uncontrollable sob as she felt the warmth and security of Billie's embrace.

"Just come back home daddy, that's all I want is for you to come back home to our family!" Billie held Nicole tightly, he now knew that this was going to be harder than he had expected and with the conversation he and Tasha had being the reason she acted out the will she did Billie felt even more guilty and like an asshole for cheating on Nicole then leaving her for one of the women he'd creep on her with.

"I'm sorry Cola, baby I'm so sorry I hurt you like that, I swear I didn't mean to I was being selfish and inconsiderate!" Billie said now holding back tears of his own as he thought of how Nicole had always been there for him through the ups and downs of life. She didn't deserve to be dog walked like he had just done her. In all honesty Nicole had been loyal and faithful to him. He was just unable to control his dick and now he was trying to wissle his way out of some bullshit that he put his self in by not considering how he was hurting the people who really loved and cared for him, and all because he didn't have any self-control. Billie took another deep breath then exhaled lost in thought holding Nicole tightly.

"Ooh Cola, I'm so ,so sorry for hurting you like this, what am I to do now? I've dug this hole for myself and now I don't know how to get myself out of it!" Billie stated out loud not realizing he was voicing his thoughts.

Nicole arched her head upward looking into Billie's eye's 'Daddy you can come back home for starters, I forgive you, I love you. We can work this out and get through this as a family. Nicole said as she began using her left hand to rub Billie's dick through his pants.

"I miss you!" Nicole moaned as she kissed Billie on his lips. Billie not able to resist Nicole sensuality parted his lips welcoming her tongue. As their tongues danced Billie grabbed Nicole's soft ass with both hands pulling her close to him which made a moan escape from Nicole as her hand found Billie's zipper they continued to kiss. Nicole released his 10 inch from its cage and began stroking him gently as they continued kissing. After several minutes Nicole broke their kiss, bit Billie's bottom lip lovingly then fell down to her knees taking all ten inches of his dick into her mouth and bobbing her head back and forward which caused Billie to moan in pleasure. Billie placed his right hand on the back of Nicole's head as Nicole sucked his dick as if it was a big stick that she'd just got off the ice cream truck on a hot sunny day, she moaned loudly loving the taste of Billie's dick as loud slurping noises escaped her mouth. Billie arched his head back in ecstasy as Nicole began massaging his balls while she deep throated his dick.

Nicole slowly pulled Billie's dick out of her mouth then ran her tongue down the shaft of his dick to his balls and sucked them gently one at a time which caused Billie knees to buckle Billie not able to handle Nicole's head game any longer pulled her up off her knees and her on top of the table. He pushed her gown up to her waist, as he slowly ran his tongue up her thigh until he got to her pussy lips. Once at her pussy lips he sucked on them hungrily, then began running his tongue around her clit as he ran two of his fingers in and out of her pussy while his thumb slide in and out her asshole. Nicole was moaning Billie's name loudly as he started sucking on her clit which caused Nicole to Shake uncontrollable as she felt herself about to have an orgasm. Nicole yelled Billie's name at the top of her lungs as she reached her orgasm and watched her juices run down Billie's chin and onto the table which turned her on and made her hornier and wetter then she already was. Billie was amazed at how much warmer and tighter Nicole's pussy was and for some reason she tasted like watermelon to him and he couldn't get enough of her. Billie began kissing his way up Nicole's body. Once at her nipples he ran his tongue around each of them, then proceed up to her neck. He placed soft kisses on her face then looked into her eyes, before he could speak Nicole slide her body slightly off the table so that her pussy could meet his dick. Nicole grabbed his dick with her right hand placing the head of his dick inside of her. Nicole worked her hips in a circle while his dick slowly entered her one inch at a time which made them both moan with pleasure as all ten inches of his dick got lost inside of her. Nicole wrapped her arms around Billie's neck then placed her legs around his waist as he cupped her soft but firm ass cheeks and lifted her completely off the table. Billie began bouncing Nicole up and down off his dick which made Nicole moan loudly on each in ward thrust Nicole would moan Billie's name so loud it echoed throughout the entire house. Billie's mouth was full he was sucking on Nicole's left nipple and enjoyed every minute of it. Nicole's breast were more defined then before and her nipples were harder than they had ever been Billie could even taste milk as he sucked on them and it was sweet as Billie continued to enjoy the taste of the milk Nicole's body was producing he wonder who was going to enjoy Nicole's milk more him or their baby. Billie began bringing Nicole up and down off his dick faster as she tightened the walls of her pussy Nicole's pussy was so good and tight that Billie had to remove her nipple from his mouth and moan her name as his knees got weak and he started cuming deep inside of her. Nicole bit into Billie's shoulder as she felt her own breath taking orgasm consuming her body. She began shaking violently as her thick cream ran down Billie's dick and balls. They held each other tightly trying to catch their breath as Billie sat Nicole on the table.

"Damn Cola!" Billie said as he tried to catch his breath. Nicole began kissing his neck then gently bit his ear.

"I really missed you daddy!" Nicole said passionately Billie's dick instantly got back hard hearing the need and longing in Nicole's voice

"Oh Cola I missed you too!" Billie moaned feeling lite headed from the sudden blood lost from his brain to his dick. Nicole feeling his hard dick up against her thigh unwrapped her legs from around his waist, kissed him then turned around and arched her back holding on to the table with both hands as she looked over her shoulder into Billie eyes

"Show me daddy, show me how much you miss me!" Nicole said seductively then licked her lips

"Show me just how much you miss this pussy!" Billie grabbed Nicole's hips and rammed all 10 inches of his dick inside of Nicole which caused her to scream his name as she dug her nails into the table holding on for dear life as Billie put a beating on her pussy that she knew he would have her sore for weeks. Nicole began rotating her hips loving every minute of it and looking forward to the soreness . . ..

Chapter 21

Monica pulled up to the Delamo Mall bang love by Keisha Cole and feeling like a million bucks. Monica had her Louis Vuitton tennis shoes with her matching Louis Vuitton sweat suit and purse. Monica was feeling out her sweat suit quite well now that she had went from a size 5 to a size 8. Monica was glowing and even with the death of her mother her skin couldn't be diminished. Monica had decided to wear her hair in a wrap like Aaliyah use to wear hers before she died. All eyes were on Monica as she entered the mall from both men and women the men were lusting while the women were hating. Monica payed no mind to either as she walked into Macys, Monica's ass was mouthwatering that several men had stop eating their food as she passed by the food court wishing they could get a bite of her. One man had even got bold enough to run over to her trying to "game her up!" Monica quickly shut him down, not even letting him finish his sentence before letting him know that she had a man and didn't think he would like or appreciate her talking to another nigga and that she respected him too much to do so, so you getting at me is a no, no so by bro!" Monica said with a smile sending the brother away with his head down and pride hurt! Monica knew to shut a nigga down quickly because if you didn't they got it in their mind that you wanted them and was just playing hard to get and wanted to be chased Monica took the escalator up to the 3rd floor of Macys headed to the infants department with a huge smile on her face thinking about all the things she wanted to buy for her and Billie's daughter. As Monica got off the escalator her cell phone rung, she looked at the caller id but the number came up as blocked Monica answered the phone as she walked over to the cribs

"Hello!" Monica said into the receiver as she looked over a beautiful oak and marble crib.

"Hi Ms. Tillis this is Markest Walben from Inglewood Mortuary, we have gotten everything together with the funeral arrangements and just need to go over them with you so if you can find the time we would like you to come in today. We are hoping to have your mother's burial by this coming Saturday or Sunday but it's completely up to you Ms. Tillis!" Monica stepped away from the crib, okay Monica said as her heart sunk thinking about her mother and wishing she was still alive so she could be shopping with her first child and her mother's first grandchild. Okay Mr. Walben I'll stop by later today what time do you close?" Monica asked feeling heavy hearted. · At 6:30 pm but I'll be here until 8:00 pm so feel free to come any time before then!" Mr. Walben said in a gentle voice.

"Okay well I'll call my fiancé and then I'll give you a call back with a definite time, thank you for calling sir!" Monica said, controlling her voice from breaking up with the sudden rush of emotions she was feeling from the loss of her mother as tears began to fall from her eyes.

"Oh no problem Ms. Tillis your mother was a wonderful person and also a good friend, I'm sorry for your loss, she will be missed god bless you!" Mr. Walben said with sincerity.

"Thank you and god bless you as well, see you soon!" Monica said then disconnected the line as she wiped her face.

"Mommy I miss you so much!" Monica said as she went through her contacts once she found the number she wanted, Monica pushed send. As the number began to ring a picture of the person being called popped up. A smile came across Monica's face as she realized she still had someone in this world that loved and needed her. As the number continued to ring her daughter gave her a strong kick to her ribs letting her know she not only had one person that needed her but she had two . . . .

Nicole was laying on Billie's chest watching him as he slept listening to his heart beat. Billie had fallen into a deep sleep shortly after laying pipe to Nicole like the plumber that he was. Nicole kissed him lovingly on his lips then snuggled back close to him, laying her head back on his chest as she thought about how much she truly loved him. Just as Nicole was starting to doze off she heard Billie's cell phone ring. Nicole ignored it, kissed Billie's chest and was slowly falling asleep when the phone began ringing again. Nicole now irritated and wanting to know who was being so damn persistent slid out of bed, careful not to wake Billie and grabbed his pants. She went into his pocket and grabbed his new galaxy 5s. The screen was locked so she couldn't see the caller's picture but the number showed as clear as day. Nicole tried to answer the call but without the passcode she couldn't. Nicole quickly grabbed a pen off the night stand and wrote down the number as the caller was now calling back for a 3rd time

"oh this gotta be some ratchet ass bitch!" Nicole said feeling the anger building up inside of her as she cut the volume down on Billie's phone so it wouldn't wake him, then placed it back in his pants pocket and put his pants back where she had gotten them. Nicole grabbed her cell phone with her left hand with the piece of paper that had the number on it tightly in her right and headed down her stair outside her bedroom. Once she was half way down the stairs she sat on them, pressed #67 to block her number then dialed the number on the paper, eagerly waiting for the bitch who was calling her man to pick up the phone so she could give her a piece of her mind.............. ....

Monica was paying for her baby's crib and Winnie the pooh accessories when her cell phone rang. Monica had called Billie three times to let him know about the arrangement that need to be made for her mother's funereal, but he didn't answer Monica thought it might be him as she grabbed her phone out her purse looking at the caller ID before she answered. The number was blocked so Monica ignored the call placing the phone back in her purse, disappointed that it wasn't Billie. Just as she was taking her hand out of her purse, her phone began ringing again. Monica looked at the caller ID again and was about to ignore the call because it was blocked when she thought to herself that it could be Billie calling from one of his boys phones. As the clerk at Macys bagged her items up, Monica pressed answer then placed the phone to her ear.

"This is Mo, what's good?" Monica said into the receiver. When she didn't get a reply Monica looked at her screen to make sure she had answered the call. Once Monica was sure she had correctly answered the phone she placed it back to her ear again.

"Hello is anybody there?" Monica asked now hearing someone breathing into the phone. Just as she was about to hang up Monica heard a women laugh into the phone then whisper

"Bitch you can never be me, so stop trying!" Monica frowned at the comment, as she was about to respond she heard the line disconnect. Monica shrugged her shoulders threw her phone back in her purse then grabbed her bags headed to her car so she could get to the funeral home, not letting the call rent any space in her mind ....

Nicole sat on the stairs lost in thought. She was in rage that Monica had called Billie's phone while they were spending time together.

"That home wrecking bitch gonna get what she got coming just like her punk ass mommy did!" Nicole thought to herself as she sat on the stairs still pissed off. Nicole got up headed back toward the bedroom where she had left Billie in bed sound asleep. She put her phone back on the dresser then crawled back in bed. Nicole wasn't going to lose Billie again, and she was going to do everything in her power to make sure he didn't leave her ,their baby or their home ever again. There's nothing that bitch can do for him that I can't!" Nicole stated as she gently pulled the sheet off of Billie body exposing his dick Nicole gently and passionately kissed his lips then whispered in his ear.

"Daddy, I'll kill over you, your mine and I'm not sharing you with no body but our child, I love you!" Billie moved in his sleep then said I love you too!" Nicole smiled then ran her tongue slowly down the center of

Billie's chest which caused soft moans to escape his lips. Once Nicole was at his dick she placed it in her wet and waiting mouth deep throating it, then pulled it out her mouth, and ran her tongue around the head of his dick. Nicole played with the head of his dick with 'her tongue for several minutes then slowly ran her tongue down the shaft, once at his balls Nicole gently sucked each of them as she pumped Billie's dick which woke him completely up.

"Damn Cola, that feels good!" Billie moaned as Nicole continued stroking his dick and sucking his balls.

"I want you to cum in my mouth daddy!" Nicole stated as she dragged her lips and tongue up and down the side of his dick sending chills down Billie's spin. Nicole run her tongue around the head of Billie's dick again, then began deep throating his dick slowly bobbing her head up and down. Billie's toes curled as Nicole started massaging his balls as she continued deep throating his dick as if it was a feeding tube and she needed to eat. Billie closed his eyes, his left hand massaged the back of Nicole's neck while his right hand held tightly to the side of the bed moaning in ecstasy as he began moving his hips with Nicole's bobbing motion.

"Oh my fucking god Cola, I'm about to cum!" Billie said as he grabbed the mattress tighter about to lose control as Nicole sped up, slowed down then sped up again all the while keeping her mouth and throat tightly wrapped around Billie's dick.

"Jesus Christ Cola, I'm cuming, oh god I'm cuming!" Billie moaned loudly as his body began jerking as he tightened his grip on the back of Nicole's head as she stop bobbing and held Billie dick in her mouth and down her throat using her jaw and throat muscles to drain him of his cum

"Fuuccccccckkkk!" Billie screamed out in pleasure as Nicole swallowed the last of his seed then slowly pulled his dick out her mouth. Nicole kissed the head of his dick tenderly then looked into his eyes.

"Big girls swallow Nicole said seductively as she crawled up toward him like a lioness looking sexy and forbidden which made Billie's dick back hard.

"I missed you daddy!" Nicole purred as she reached Billie's lips still looking him in his eyes as she kissed him.

"I missed you to Cola Billie said as Nicole reached back with her left hand grabbing Billie's dick as she slowly set on it moaning as all 10 inches of his dick got lost inside her wet tight pussy.

"Show me daddy!' Nicole said as she placed her hands on his chest and began riding Billie's dick as if she was a jockey and his dick was a thorough bred horse

"Show me that you miss this pussy!" Nicole moaned through clenched teeth as Billie grabbed her hips and started thrusting his hips upward, trying to write his name in Nicole's pussy . . . .

Tasha had ten minutes before clocking out from work. She texted Nicole after shutting down her computer:

Cola, I'm about to get off work let me know what time you want to meet up at Wal-Mart, I'ma stop at Johnny Pastrami and pick me up something to eat let me know if you want something.......Love you, Tee.

Tasha sent the text, grabbed her purse out her bottom desk drawer kicked it closed and headed out her office toward the elevator. As she got on the elevator her phone began to ring. Tasha answered it on the second ring, after looking at the caller I D.

"Good afternoon, how can I help you!" Tasha said sounding cheerful.

"Hi this is Eddie from Game stop in Inglewood my I speak to Tasha Ward please!" This is she how are you Eddie?" Tasha asked as the elevator doors closed and she pressed 1 for the first floor.

"I'm fine!" Eddie said as Tasha stepped out the elevator grabbed her time card and clocked out.

"I'm calling to let you know the game you pre-ordered Assassins creed IV black flad is here for pick up, you can get it whenever you like oh yeah your Xbox one is also here!" Tasha smiled to herself

"Thank you Eddie you made my day!" Tasha stated smiling from ear to ear as she walked to her car.

"I'll swing by in about 45 minutes, you just made my day!" Well I'm glad I could make you smile, if you can't make it in 45 minutes it's okay we close at 9:00 pm, I'll be here until then! Eddie said as he rung up a customer

"Oh I'll be there but, thank you, I'll see you shortly!' Tasha stated as she got into her car. Alrighty then see you in a few!" Eddie said then disconnected the line focusing on the customer in front of him. Tasha started her car smiling from ear to ear thinking how happy Billie would be the next time he came over and seen a Xbox one and the game she'd bought for him hooked up and ready to be played. Tasha pulled out her jobs parking lot onto Carson St. head to the 91 freeway so she could get her something to eat and go get her baby daddy's new toy too in hopes that it would keep him around her house and with her longer . ...

Monica was getting off the 105 freeway headed down Prairie Ave to the Inglewood Cemetery when she decided to text Billie because he still hadn't returned her call or answered her message yet Monica began texting as she waited at a red light on Prairie and Century:

Daddy I'm on my way to make the arrangements for mommies funereal, if you can please make it there, I could use your support right now! I love you so much daddy and hope to see you soon Love Mo

Monica sent the text as the light turned green and sat her phone on the passenger seat as she began driving she said a silent prayer asking god to let Billie get her text and respond letting her know he was on his way because she needed him right now as Monica passed Arbor Vida her hands tightened on the steering wheel thinking about how her mother was killed in cold blood. Monica took a deep breath exhaled then regained her composure knowing that she would need Billie's shoulder to cry on at the cemetery because this would be the hardest thing she ever had to do. ....

Nicole was lying on Billie's chest listening to his heart beat as he slept. Nicole had put him to sleep and drained him of all his energy for some reason Nicole was hornier then a dog in heat, she had road Billie until he had released his seed inside of her then Nicole topped it off by sucking his dick until he was back at his full 10 inches and making him cum in her mouth. Suck him completely dry and taking the remaining of his energy which put him in deep coma like sleep. Nicole was just about to doze off

when she heard Billie's phone going off again. Nicole kissed his chest the crawled out of bed retrieving it out his pocket once again. This time Nicole noticed it was a text instead of a call. Nicole now determined to open Billie's phone tried to unlock it by entering his birthday. ("that is not the correct password, please try again!") The screen read which frustrated Nicole. She took a moment to think, she tried his last four of his social, within seconds the same massage appeared Nicole took a deep breath then exhaled, she knew this was the last time she could try because after four wrong passcode entrees the phone would lock up and Billie would know she had been fucking with his phone while he was asleep. Nicole stood over the bed staring at Billie with the phone in her hand. After a few minutes she smiled to herself Nicole entered the year they had graduated from High School, the screen opened up telling her how many missed calls and texts he had. Nicole laughed to herself as she leaned over the bed giving Billie a lite kiss on the lips.

"I know you so well she stated in a whisper!" then walked out the room reading Billie's texts.

Once Nicole was half way down the stairs she sat down, her stomach turned as she read Monica's text.

"Bitch fuck what you going through Billie ain't going to be there for you now or ever!" Nicole stated as an idea came to her head. She responded to Monica's text with a devilish smile on her face. After sending the text Nicole waited for a reply. Once she received the reply she erased all of Monica's text plus the one she went with the reply then quickly ran up the stairs replacing Billie's phone back in his pocket.

"Nobody is ever taking my family away from me again!" Nicole stated as she got 3 Ambiens out the bathroom cabinet then crushed them up to dust.

"I got something for you scandalous ass bitch!" Nicole thought to herself as she shot down the stairs and into the kitchen with the crushed pills in a napkin. Nicole put the crushed ambiens in a zip lock bag then picked up her house phone calling the soul food cafe on La Brea and Mancaster ordering smothered fried chicken, greens, mac and cheese and hot water com bread. The person taking the order told Nicole that her food would be ready in 10 minutes. Nicole gave them her name, phone number then hung up and ran back upstairs checking on Billie. Once she was sure he was still sound asleep Nicole threw on some juicy sweat pants with the matching jacket zipped it up, slipped her feet in her white air force ones then tied them up. Once dressed she went back downstairs grabbed her keys and phone headed out the door to get Billie's food before he woke up. Nicole was on a time schedule, she looked at her watch realizing she only had 30 minutes to work with so there was no time to play ....

Monica was at the red light on Florence about to tum into the entrance to the cemetery when she received Billie's text. A smile came on her face as she read it:

Hey baby, sorry it took me so long to respond, I'll be there in like 45 mins. I'm with Zane helping him move. Get you something to eat and meet me in front of the cemetery at 4:45 I love you Billie

Monica pussy got wet damn

"I love this nigga she stated to herself as she replied to Billie's text:

Okay Daddy, I love you too, Ima stop and get me and our baby something to eat from Applebee's, I can't wait to see you, I miss you I'll be waiting for you at the cemetery I love you so much Kisses and hugs Mo

Monica sent the text as she passed the cemetery up then made a quick u-tum. As she turned back on Prairie head toward Century a smile came across her face. Monica cut her Keisha Cole *CD* on and played Love singing alone with her favorite female artist feeling in her heart that as long as she had Billie and their baby everything would be alright. ....

Nicole had made it to the soul food cafe and back home in 10 minutes flat. She had read Tasha's text at a red light and responded telling her to meet her at Wal-Mart in downtown Long Beach at about 6:00 pm. Nicole sat Billie's food on the kitchen counter the shot up the stairs like a rocket to checking on him. Nicole smiled to herself as she stood in the doorway to their bedroom seeing he was still sound asleep. Nicole quickly pulled off her air force one's and her juicy sweat suit. Now buck naked she gave Billie a soft kiss then went back down stairs to the kitchen. Once back in the kitchen Nicole placed Billie's food on a plate then grabbed the zip lock bad she's put the Ambien in, opened it up and mixed a little in with the yams and greens. After she mixed the Ambien in good enough so it wouldn't be detected, Nicole grabbed a glass pouring the remaining of the bag's contents inside the cup.· She then opened the fridge, grabbed the Hawaiian punch and poured Billie a nice tall glass of his favorite drink. Nicole put the container back in the frig then grabbed 3 cubs of ice out the freezer. She closed the frig, dropped the ice cubes in the cup of Hawaiian punch used a spoon to stir it up, then placed a fork on Billie's plate. Nicole put the plate of food and the drink on a bed tray and took the food upstairs. Once upstairs Nicole sat the tray on the night stand and grabbed his phone out his pants pocket, she unlocked it and read his latest text from Monica"

Daddy I'm at Applebee's waiting to be seated, I didn't realize how hungry I was till I smelled food =) I love you and will see you shortly Mo

Nicole looked over at Billie then began texting Monica back as if she was Billie:

Hay daddy's angel, can't wait to see you too, I might be a little late, no more than 10 or 15 minutes so take your time eating, my phone is dying and my car charger isn't working so this will be my last text I love you and will see you at the cemetery around 5:15 pm know later then 5:30pm. Enjoy your dinner Daddy

Nicole sent the text then erased the text from Monica and her reply when it was confirmed that it was sent. Nicole placed Billie's cell phone back in his pants pocket then sat next to him on the bed. She kissed him on his lips passionately then whispered in his ear

"wake up daddy!" As she reached under the covers grabbing his dick and gently stroking it up and down.

"Come on daddy wake up for me!" Nicole purred as she felt his dick starting to grow in his hands. Billie's eyes slowly opened as a smile came across his face.

"Hmmmm, you sure know how to wake a nigga up, don't you?" Billie asked

loving how her hand felt around his dick as she slowly stroked him.

"You know I got you daddy, but before I get you all riled up I made you some food!" Nicole stated as she got up off the bed, headed toward the dresser. Billie looked at her ass giggle as she walked to the dresser grabbing the tray. Nicole brought the tray back to the bed then set it across his lap.

"Damn Cola, you been busy while I was asleep!" Billie stated as he looked over the food licking his lips.

"I sure have, I have to keep my daddy energized. Now you eat up!" Nicole said giving Billie a mouthful of greens. Emmmm Em!" Billie moaned as he chewed the greens.

"Damn I missed your cooking Cola!" Billie said as he chewed the greens. Nicole smiled

"Here take this fork feed yourself while I give you a reason to hurry up and finish your food Nicole stated as she slide under the covers and started sucking Billie's dick just as he put a fork full of yams in his mouth. Billie

moaned in pleasure at the taste of the candy yams and the sensation he was getting as Nicole deep throated his dick which made his toes curl. Billie eyes rolled into the back of his head as he took down another mouthful of greens getting 2 of the things that any man loves, some good food and some good head ....

Tasha had gotten her pastrami special with a pineapple shake and was now sitting in her car eating her food in the parking lot of Johnny Pastrami's. Tasha finished her Pastrami, threw the wrapper out the window wiped her hands on a napkin then started her car, she smiled as she backed up then put her car in drive headed to game stop to go get Billie's Xbox 1 and the game she had pre-ordered. Tasha was eating a onion ring as she turned on Crenshaw, she looked at her Chanel watch and notice it was only 4:38 pm Tasha was making good time and was excited about meeting up with Nicole later to go shopping and couldn't wait to be back in her best friends company. Tasha ate another onion ring then took a sip of her shake as she waited for the light to tum green on Crenshaw and Florence. Just as the light turned green Tasha cut on her K. Michelle CD

and cut the volume up to 30 as very special began playing throughout the car. Tasha started singing along with K. Michelle feeling what she was saying as a blue BMW 745 tried to catch up to her. Tasha in her own world not paying the car nor the driver any attention went around the turns that lead to the light on Western and Crenshaw doing 70 swaying her head to the music still singing. She stopped at the light still singing as Zane pulled alongside of her and blew his horn to get her attention. Hearing the horn Tasha looked over with an attitude wondering who had the nerve to be blowing at her and was about to give them a piece of her mind when she realized who it was. Tasha rolled down her window smiling from ear to ear.

"Hay Zane, what it do boy!" Tasha said over her Bose system in her car. Zane smiled

"Girl, you was flying around those curves I been trying to get your attention since Florence, how's everything been? Zane asked as he took a quick look in his rear view mirror.

"It's been okay, what about you how's things going?" Tasha asked still smiling

"oh I'm good maintaining, I've been a little worried about our knuckle head homie boy Billie, a nigga haven't heard from him in like 3 days and that's not like him!" Zane said with concern as someone blew their horn letting them both know the light was green and they were holding up traffic. Zane pointed toward the shell gas station across the light then pulled off Tasha quickly got behind him and followed him into the gas station parking lot. They both parked by the water and air pump then hoped out their cars giving each other a hug.

"Damn girl, you look good, with your fine ass and you glowing! Zane stated looking Tasha over and smiling.

"Shut up nigga and thank you for the compliment, you know I'm pregnant right?" Tasha asked as she looked into his eyes waiting for a response. Zane's jaw dropped.

"Your what? Who got my boo thang knocked?" Zane asked jokingly. Tasha playful socked him in his right arm "none of your business!" Tasha said smiling

"and you can stop worrying about Billie because he's okay, you know he went to Cancun on a business trip, that's more than likely the reason you haven't heard from him!" Tasha said checking her surroundings then looking back at Zane.

"Oh yeah, he did tell me about that, but after what happened at his and Nicole's house I was so concerned I just forgot about him leaving thinking he needed his space so he could think!" Zane stated then looked at his watch

"So how is Cola holding up, I been trying to call her but she send a nigga straight to voice mail!"

"Oh she good, I'm supposed to meet her in an hour or so, I'll tell her to call you!" Zane smiled,

"You do that and if you talk to Billie tell him I'ma fuck his ass up if he don't check in soon, even though you said he good the crew is still worried!" Zane said as he gave her a hug then kissed her on the cheek,

"I gotta go get my son from day care, tell that nigga that got you pregnant, he better do his job or Ima come see about him!" Zane said looking at her seriously. Tasha waved him off

"Boy shut up and go get Zalen!" Tasha stated laughing as Zane hopped in his car

"Love you sis!" Zane said as he pulled off cutting his music up

Tasha shook her head still smiling

"love you too drive save!" Tasha said as she got in her car headed back toward game stop wondering how Billie's boys all of whom she went to school with and looked at as brothers was going to take it when they found out that she was carrying his baby. Tasha turned out of the gas station headed toward Century lost in thought wondering what would the crew think ....

Chapter 22

Nicole's plans to put Billie to sleep had worked better and faster than she had planned. Billie had only ate one piece of chicken, half the yams, all the greens and drunk the Hawaiian punch before he was sound asleep. Nicole hearing his breathing change looked up from sucking his dick and noticed Billie knocked out with the fork still in his hand. Nicole smiled to herself as she rolled out the bed then grabbed the bed tray from over him, sitting it on the dresser. Nicole kissed him on the lips then pulled the covers over his body

"I love you daddy, you get your rest I'll be back before you ever know or realize I was gone!" Nicole gave Billie another kiss then hoped off the bed. She threw on her black fitted tights with her Jordan fitted shirt which was also black then slipped her feet into her pink and black Jordan running shoes. Nicole tied her Jordan's up then grabbed her phone and car keys. As she walked out the bedroom door she looked over her shoulder taking a quick glance at Billie

"I'm not losing you again!" She stated as she pulled the bedroom door up then went down the stairs two at a time. Once down stairs Nicole went into the hall closet and grabbed her Prada shoe box pulling her smith and Western 9mm out of it. She put the box back in the closet closed the door then slapped the clip into her gun. Nicole chocked the hammer then put the gun on safety.

"This is my family," Nicole said as she put her gun in her purse and I'm not letting nothing or no one destroy it!" She stated as she walked out her front

door closing and locking it behind herself. Nicole got in her car placing her purse on the passenger seat, she looked at the time on her phone it was 5: 10 pm Nicole started her car then backed out her driveway, she put her game face on as she put her car in drive. As Nicole hit La

Tieara, hoping on the 405 freeway. She cut on her DMX CD. Nicole got on the freeway singing alone with DMX going 75, as she repeated the words DMX spoke Nicole smiled replacing the words with her on 1, 2 Nicole is coming for you 3, 4 you better lock your door 5, 6 get your crucifix 7, 8 don't stay up late 9, 10 I'm about to kill again she stated with a devilishly smile on her face as she switched freeways and merged into traffic on the 105 head to the Inglewood cemetery . . ..

Monica had finished eating and was getting into her car leaving Applebee's feeling brand new with a smile on her face. While at Applebee' s Monica had eaten lobster tails, fried shrimp boiled broccoli with cheese sauce, steamed vegetables, brown rice with a Caeser salad for desert Monica had a slice of double chocolate cake with a scoop of vanilla ice cream. After Monica had ate her food, she took the liberty of ordering Billie the same meal, except she replaced the Lobster tails with a juicy steak and decide the ice cream would melt so she just got him a slice of cake. As Monica closed her car door, she sat Billie's food on the passenger seat glancing at the time on her cars console. Seeing that it was 5:15 pm she quickly started her car, put it in reverse pulling out the parking spot then threw her BMW X5 in drive headed to the cemetery. Monica pulled onto Century driving toward Prairie Ave doing 60 MPH she wanted to be there when Billie got there so she could greet him with dinner, a hug and a kiss showing her appreciation for him being there for her. Monica got to Prairie Ave and made a right, just as take it to the head" By Rick Ross Nikki Minaj Lil Wayne and Trey Songz came on her car stereo system. Monica smiled to herself as she realized that Prairie Ave didn't have a lot of traffic and she would be at the cemetery in minutes. Monica cut the music up in her car singing along with Nikki Minaj as she drove down Prairie Ave eager to see her man. Their daughter kicked as she thought about Billie

"Okay I know you want to see, well hear your daddy too!" Monica said as she rubbed her stomach smiling waiting for the light to turn green on Larch. Monica was amazed at how alert their baby was, also at how this little girl in her stomach seemed to know her daddy's name.

Monica believed this because whenever she would say Billie's name or think about him too long, their daughter would kick or move around. Monica smiled as she pulled into the cemetery.

"Ima ask your daddy can we name you after your grandmother!" Monica said as she rubbed her stomach parking her car on the west end of the cemetery. Monica cut her engine off then placed both her hands on her stomach.

"What do you think about that, would you like me and your daddy to name you after your grandma" Monica asked stroking her stomach gently Monica felt

a double kick a tear fell from her eyes as she smiled,

"Well I guess that's a yes huh?" Monica asked still stroking her stomach knowing that her and Billie were going to have their hands full when their daughter was born and wishing her mom was here so she could tell her how smart her grandchild was. Monica felt two kicks and began laughing to herself now thinking that she was losing her mind because she felt her unborn child was communicating her with. Monica took a deep breath then exhaled

"Okay, I know I'm not crazy!" Monica said out loud then looked down at her stomach

"If you can understand me kick twice!" Monica said still looking at her stomach with both hands stroking it lightly

"See, I knew I......." Monica felt two kicks before she could finish her sentence. Her mouth opens in shock

"Oh god this can't be real!" Monica stated out loud staring at her stomach in amazement,

"Okay, okay just to confirm your mommy's doubtful mind, answer one more question for me!" Monica said still in disbelieve

"if you love your daddy give me one kick!" As soon a Monica finished her question she felt one of the most powerful kicks she'd felt since their baby had started kicking

"Okay, okay I believe!" Monica looked around the parking lot still rubbing her stomach praying silently that Billie would hurry up and get there because she not only wanted to tell him what happened Monica wanted him to witness it for himself Monica continued rubbing her stomach as she waited for Billie to pull up still amazed at what their unborn child had just done...................

Nicole pulled into the cemetery parking lot driving slowly. She pulled her gun out of her purse and placed it across her lap as she scanned the parking lot trying to spot Monica's car. Just as she was about to turn in to the southeast parking lot Nicole spotted Monica's car parked in the southwest lot near the entrance closes to Western. Nicole rolled down her window and decided to try to creep up from behind Monica's car. She took her foot completely off the gas as she made a quick right turning into the parking lot that Monica's car was sitting in. Nicole's mind raced as she got closer and closer to the back of Monica's car. Soon they'll be burying you next to your mother you home racking bitch, I'm about to make sure of that!" Nicole sated as she closed in on the back of Monica's BMW *X5*. Nicole picked up her gun off her lap looking around to make sure the parking lot was clear of potential witnesses and innocent bystanders. Nicole was about 100 yards away when she was certain that the coast was clear. A devilish grin came across her face as she gripped the handle of the gun tighter

"Today you'll get what you deserve!" Nicole said as she prepared herself for what she was about to do. 'Today you're going to be held responsible for fucking with my family, today you're going to pay for trying to take my life!" Nicole stated now 50 yards away from her next victim whom she considered her prey . ...

Monica looked up from rubbing her stomach and notice Billie's jag slowly approaching in her rear view mirror. Monica smiled to herself as she pulled the driver side visor down then looked in the mirror as she placed on some lip gloss then adjusted her hair once satisfied that she looked good Monica closed the visor then looked through her rear view mirror again, noticing that Billie was even closer.

"Your daddy is here!" Monica said rubbing her stomach

with a smile on her face. As Monica was opening the door to get out the car she could greet Billie with a kiss and a hug after he parked and got out his car their daughter kicked Monica giggled

"Yeah know I know, I'm glad to see him too!" She stated as she stepped out the car ready to share with Billie how smart and alert their baby was ....

Nicole was about 15 yards away from Monica's car when she noticed the driver's side door opening

"Fuck!" Nicole yelled as she watched Monica stepping out the car smiling. Nicole slammed her food on the gas and her Jaguar shot forward she quickly stuck her gun out the window and began unloading rounds toward Monica as she closed the few yards between them ....

Monica noticed something was wrong when she heard the engine revving and saw the car moving toward her like a rocket. Monica quick on her feet dived back into the car as she heard gun fire come from the direction of the car speeding toward her. She covered her head as she heard her driver's side window being shot out and bullet after bullet hit her driver's side door which she had left open

"What the fuck is going on!" Monica thought to herself as she reached and opened her glove compartment grabbing her 40 Cal Ruger and its clip as the car that Monica had thought was Billie's flew by her open door. Monica slammed her clip into her gun pulled the hammer then closed her door she quickly started her car throwing it in drive in pursuit of whom ever had just tried not only to take her life but also her unborn baby's. Monica watched the car drive out of the cemetery going 60 turning onto Western

"Whoever that was got me fucked up!"

Monica said as she pulled out of the cemetery with her gun on her lap. She spotted the Jag at the light on Prairie and once seeing the plates knew immediately whose car it was

"Oh this bitch got me fucked up, she done tried to sneak up and take me out, you done fucked with the wrong bitch!" Monica stated, keeping a 3 car distance from Nicole. Monica felt her daughter kick and was relieved to know that their baby was okay. Monica followed Nicole down Prairie waiting for her chance to make Nicole regret not making sure she had killed her.

Nicole was pissed as she texted Tasha telling her to meet her at Wal-Mart while she got on the 105 freeway headed toward the 710 freeway. Nicole replayed the shooting at the cemetery in her head and smiled as she remembered seeing Monica fall into the car

"I shot that bitch!" Nicole stated to herself, as she switched lanes then sent the text to Tasha

"Why did her stupid ass have to get out the car!" Nicole stated to herself as she got on the 405 now second guessing herself, wishing she had doubled back an made sure she had killed Monica's crafty ass. Nicole had planned to walk up to the car or pull up to the driver's side window and dome Monica

"This stupid bitch fucked my plan up!" Nicole thought to herself as her phone went off with a reply text from Tasha saying ("Okay I'm on my way!") Nicole smiled to herself knowing that if Monica wasn't dead and things went bad, Monica never had seen her face and she had a full proof

Alibi. She was at home having sex with her soon to be husband and once he was fed and sound asleep she called her best friend and they went shopping at Wal-Mart. Tasha would confirm this without a doubt, without a shadow of a doubt! A evil grin came across Nicole's face as she cut on her car stereo system playing her favorite song by Dr. Dre 'Bitch Niggas', feeling like she was on top of the world and couldn't be touched, never realizing that Monica was tailing her …. ………………

Chapter 23

Tasha had made it to game stop on Century Ave and Village way in the Inglewood Shopping Center at 5:30 pm. She was putting Billie's Xbox 1 with the games she'd bought in the trunk of her car smiling from ear to ear thinking about how Billie was going to enjoy his new system while Tasha was in game stop she ended up buying Billie two other games with the one she had pre-ordered. This was because once she'd got to the store and was paying for her items Eddie the sales rep began telling her about the newest Call of Duty Ghost which she knew Billie would love and a fighting game called Marvel vs. D C Commies that she picked because she want to whip Billie's ass, and one of the D C Comic characters she could be was Wonder Women.

Tasha was getting into her car when her phone went off letting her know she had a new text massage. Tasha smiled as she read Nicole's text:

On my way to Wal-Mart sis, can't wait to see you. There's a little traffic on the 710, but I'll be there soon (SO GET YO ASS HERE!) =) Love Cola.

Tasha quickly responded. "Okay, on my way!" Then started her car, she pulled out on Ukon and made a left on to Century headed toward Prairie Ave. Tasha cut on her Future CD and began playing her favorite song featuring Kelly Roland (It'll Never End) Tasha was feeling herself as she turned on to the 105 freeway singing along with Kelly Roland headed toward Long Beach so she could meet her sister and best friend at Wal-Mart so they could do some shopping and hopefully find some common ground. Tasha relaxed in her seat as she changed from the 105 to the 710 freeway and merged into traffic thinking about all the things she wanted to get from Wal-Mart for her baby while she was there and how good it would be for her and Nicole to be hanging out together again.............

Monica was still in pursuit of her shooter. As she drove on the 710 freeway 3 cars behind the person that not only tried to kill her but also her unborn child it was crystal clear to Monica who the shooter was.

"This bitch tried to really kill me!" Monica said as she let another car get in front of her widening the distance. Monica rubbed her stomach as she watched Nicole's

Jaguar switch lanes about to exit on Pacific Ave. Monica waited till she felt Nicole was a safe distance away from her before she switched lanes still keeping a four car distances as they both got off the freeway Monica remembering the reputation of the Long Beach Police, prayed that she wouldn't get pulled over because of the shot out window and the bullet holes in her driver's door.

"As soon as I get a clear shot Ima take this punk bitch out, fuck playing I'm not going to give this bitch another chance to try to take out me or mines!" Monica stated as she watched the Jag turn on Pine Ave. Monica began thinking about Billie and the text she'd received that had her at the cemetery at just the right time for Nicole to try what she had done.

"Oh my god, this bitch got Billie's phone or had it, shit but how did she get it? Does she have my daddy hostage, maybe she stole it maybe she....." Monica let go of her thoughts momentarily as she watched the Jaguar pull into the underground parking lot at Wal-Mart. She had to keep driving straight because if she didn't she would of ended up directly behind Nicole and that would of blown her cover. As Monica passed by all her assumptions was confirmed of Nicole being the one that shot at her as she watched Nicole grab a ticket then drove into the parking lot.

"I got yo number bitch!" Monica stated as she bust a u-tum then pulled into the underground parking lot herself. As she drove in she checked her magazine then slammed it into her 40 Cal

"This time it's more than personal!" Monica stated as she parked her car scanning the parking lot for Nicole's Jag. Monica said a quick prayer, hoping that Billie was okay because if he wasn't she would completely lose her mind. Monica spotted Nicole and sat in silence waiting for the right moment to take Nicole out, but first she decided she would question Nicole about Billie's phone and how the fuck she had gotten it. ....

Chapter 24

Tasha was listening to Chris Brown and Aaliyah's new hit single (How do they know) as she pulled into the underground parking lot at Wal-Mart. Tasha was still feeling good about meeting with Nicole and was in her own world as she parked . Tasha cut her car off then called Nicole, Nicole picked up on the first right.

"Hey girl I'm here!" Tasha said smiling from ear to ear.

"Damn bitch, it took you long enough I been waiting for you for twenty minutes!" Nicole lied trying to get her alibi flawless

"Where you at?" Nicole asked smiling to herself at how she had got away with another murder.

"I'm in the parking lot about to get out my car, where you at bitch?" Tasha asked happy to be talking and spending time with her best friend like they use to and hoping they could get through this.

"Shit I was sitting in my car playing candy crush waiting for yo stank ass!" They shared a laugh. 'Bitch meet me at the front entrance. Nicole said as she got out the car.

"I'll see you in a second!" Nicole hung up her phone laughing to herself as she realized how much she missed Tasha even with the betrayal Nicole still loved her girl

"I might let this bitch live Nicole thought as the line was disconnected. Tasha was smiling from ear to ear as she got out her car closed her door then pressed her alarm on her key ring. Just as Tasha began walking toward the exit of the parking lot she heard several gun shots. Tasha quickly took cover behind her car wondering who was shooting in the parking lot at Wal-Mart and hoping Nicole was okay...........

Just as Nicole was putting her phone in her purse and walking toward the exit of the parking lot she noticed Monica walking toward her with a gun in her left hand, with no time to think Nicole dived behind the car parked next to her, quickly pulling her 9mm out her purse and letting off 3 shots in the direction that she saw Monica coming from.

"What the fuck is this bitch still doing alive!" Nicole thought to herself as she tried to regain her breath

"This bitch has to be a descendent of cat woman because I know I saw her slumped over." Nicole stated to herself as she looked over the hood of the BMW 745 she had dived behind for a shield and searched the parking lot for movement in the direction she had seen Monica coming from. Nicole now realizing not doubling back at the cemetery was her biggest mistake and began worrying about how she was going to get herself out of this situation.

"Fuck, fuck, fuck!" Nicole stated in frustration as she looked underneath the BMW she was still using for cover to see if she could see a body lying down where she'd seen Monica coming from or if Monica was using the cars in that direction to hide behind. Seeing no trace of Monica, Nicole took a deep breath, exhaled then counted to three and stood up, quickly walking to the exit of the parking lot trying to get to the safety of Walmart and all the people inside the store

"Ima call the police and tell them that this bitch just tried to kill me because my fiancé just decided to leave her alone and she feels if I'm out the way he'll come back to her!" Nicole thought to herself smiling as she placed her gun in her purse. Just as she was about to walk through the exit of the parking lot she heard someone call her name, Nicole not bothering to look back took off running toward the entrance to Wal-Mart. Nicole was 15 feet away from the double doors to the store when she heard

3 shots as Nicole said a silent prayer hoping the bullets would miss her she was knocked off her feet, landing face first on the ground.

Nicole's body felt like it was on fire she tried to get up but her legs wouldn't cooperate. As Nicole opened her mouth to call for help she looked up to see the doors for Walmart repeatedly opening and closing welcoming her into the store, she passed out before the word help ever escaped her lips ......

Monica thinking quickly did a front roll behind a Impala when she saw Nicole draw her gun. Monica moved swiftly in between the parked cars going away from Nicole hoping she hadn't seen her, knowing Nicole would be looking for a body or some form of life after the 3 shots she had fired. Monica found an Infinity Q45 about 35 feet away from the exit and silently waited there planning her next move and watching the car she'd seen Nicole dive behind. After a few minutes, Monica noticed Nicole quickly making her way toward the exit of the parking lot Monica called Nicole's name hoping to get her attention but instead of looking back Nicole took off running. Monica not wanting to let Nicole get away again pulled her gun from her waistband and let off 3 shots. As Monica saw Nicole falling, she turned on her heels headed towards her car ....

After 2 minutes had passed and Tasha hadn't heard any shots being fired she stood up looking around the parking lot making sure it was clear before she moved from her hiding spot. Tasha noticed Nicole walking out of the exit and smiled. Just as Tasha was about to start walking toward the exit herself she heard a woman voice calling Nicole and saw Nicole start running after hearing her name. As Tasha wondered why Nicole started running she heard 2 gun shots. Tasha screamed at the top of her lungs as she saw the 3 bullets hit Nicole and watched her fall face first. Tasha quickly scanned the parking lot again now in the direction she heard the gun shots come from as she pulled her 38 snub nose from her purse. Tasha saw the shooter looking over their shoulder while making her get away toward the rear of the parking lot and let off two shots from her 38, as the person ducked for cover behind a hummer. Whoever this person was had balls of steel as Tasha notice them stand back up and look directly at her feeling whomever it was, was about to take a shot at her so she let off another round which made the shooter disappear as the driver side window of the Hummer shattered. Tasha in a state of hysteria put her gun back in her purse then ran over to Nicole's side. Tears ran freely down Tasha's face as she looked in her best friends eyes since childhood and grabbed her hand

"I'm here Cola!" Tasha said as a crowd of people began to surround them.

"I'm so sorry Cola!" Tasha stated in between sobs still holding Nicole's hand tightly

"Sis you have to hold on, you have to be okay, you can't die, I need you, we have to go shopping for my baby, your niece or nephew we have to decorate his or her room, Cola you have to hold on please, I can't do this without you!" Tasha begged as her tears began to blur her vision.

"Somebody get me some mutha·fuck'in help!" Tasha screamed at all the people standing around her and Nicole with their hands over their mouths some in disbelief while other where in shock. Nicole gave a half smile

"It's okay Tee it's going to be okay!" Nicole stated in a low tone that only Tasha could hear.

"I love you and I forgive you for fucking Billie,

"Nicole said then took a minute to catch her breath.

"I was so mad at you, but I missed you more," Nicole said with tears in her eyes.

"I'm glad you're here with me!" Nicole stated then began

coughing uncontrollably. Tasha now in an emotional reek, began rambling

"I....I was so stupid, I shouldn't of betrayed you I was not.. ..." Nicole cut her off by holding up her other hand.

"What's done is done, we can't change the past sis!" Nicole said then smiled

"Just promise you won't leave me and if I don't make it, that you'll look after him for me." Nicole stated then tried to catch her breath Tasha grabbed Nicole's hand tighter I promise Cola and I'm not going nowhere!" Tasha stated in tears,

"I fuckin got you Cola, just hold on for me!" Tasha said as she watched the ambulance pull up and the medic's jumped out running their way. Tasha began rubbing Nicole's headsoftly

"There here, I told you I got you sis, now just hold on Cola, bad bitches don't die!" Tasha stated as the medics knelled down next to them and quickly put an IV into Nicole's arm while the other two medics began putting her on a gurney. As they began to roll Nicole toward the ambulance she pulled Tasha close to her and whispered in her ear

"Monica is the one that shot me!" Nicole stated then kissed Tasha on her cheek and I'm pregnant too" Nicole stated as the medic made Nicole let Tasha go then pulled her away. Tasha stood there in front of Wal-Mart in total shock, as they put Nicole in the ambulance

"Monica shot you!" Tasha repeated to herself as she remembered the shooter turning around and looking at her.

"Monica!" Tasha stated out loud, then the second thing Nicole told her hit her like a ton of bricks

"You're pregnant!" Tasha stated out loud making the people around her look at her like she had just lost her mind. Tasha was snapped out of her trans as one of the medics snapped his fingers in her face

"Hello Ma' am are you okay?" He asked, with concern in his voice.

"Yeah I'm fine, just a little shook up!" Tasha responded.

"Well that's completely understandable after what you've just witnessed. But we need to get your sister to the hospital, the bullets she took damaged her spinal cord and she is hemorrhaging. We need to know if your riding with us or not!" The medic asked as he walked over to the ambulance then climbed in.

"Yes!" Tasha answered still a little shook up from the

information that Nicole had told her. The medic helped Tasha into the back of the ambulance then closed the doors.

Tasha grabbed Nicole's hand and sat down next to her. The medic gave two hard knocks on the back door and the ambulance took off with the sirens blasting headed to Long Beach Memorial Hospital ....

Monica was making her way toward her car when she heard a woman screaming

"No!" She quickly glanced into the direction she heard the scream from. Monica was shocked when she noticed it was Tasha and picked up her step trying to avoid Tasha noticing her. Monica got a few more cars away from the incident and took a quick look over her shoulder to see Tasha pointing a gun at her. Monica ducked down behind a hummer and heard two shots being fired in her direction. Not one to except being shot at Monica swiftly stood up looking toward Tasha reaching into her waistband. Just as Monica was about to let off a shot of her own Tasha let off another round. Monica ducked down once again as the driver's side window of the Hummer shattered. Monica knowing that Tasha was only trying to protect her friend and didn't have anything to do with her and Nicole's beef, decided to let Tasha be. Monica stayed low, moving in between the cars. Once at her vehicle she quickly hit her alarm then hopped in. Monica took a look around the park lot for camera's as she started her car, once she was satisfied that there wasn't any she slowly pulled out of the parking structure onto 3rd Ave, as the Long Beach Police flew down Pine toward the front of Wal-Mart. Monica kept her composure and said a silent prayer. She drove up 3rd Ave till she got to Pacific Ave.

Once at Pacific Av Monica made a left on the green light then drove down Pacific until she got to Ocean Ave and made a right headed to the 710 freeway. Once on the 710 freeway she thought about the chain of events that had just taken place.

"Better her than me Monica said as she rubbed her stomach, she remembered something that her daddy had told her when he first taught her to use a gun

"Guns don't kill people, people kill people. If you ever pull a gun on someone you better use it and don't hesitate because best believe they won't hesitate when they pull it on you!" Monica smiled at the words of wisdom from her father. She then remembered why she wanted to talk to Nicole and tried to call Billie, his phone went straight to voicemail.

Monica rubbed her stomach

"We gotta find your daddy and hope that crazy bitch didn't kill him!" Monica said as she merged into traffic on the 710 freeway. She felt her daughter kick in agreeance with her as she remembered the app Billie had installed on her phone. Monica activated the app on her phone that linked with Billie's Jaguars GPS and waited as her phone searched for the location of Billie's car. Monica didn't feel a bit of guilt for taking Nicole's life, because she knew that if she hadn't taken hers, Nicole would of for sure killed her and Monica wasn't going out like that. She had too much to live for. Monica smiled to herself as her phone found the location of Billie's car and began guiding her there.

Monica said a prayer hoping Billie was okay as she followed her phones GPS to his cars location.

Chapter 25

Billie was woken up by the sound of loud banging at his and Nicole's front door. As he tried to get out of bed he felt dizzy. He called out for Nicole but there was no answer. He slowly got up, put his pants on then headed down the stairs holding on to the rail for support.

"Who is it?" Billie asked as he took a minute to regain his balance, feeling like the world was spinning. Once sure he wouldn't fall he walked down the last of the stairs and to the front door. LA County Sheriff Department, a man's voice said from behind the door

"Sheriff!" Billie repeated to his self as he opened to door and seen 6 sheriff deputies with two plain clothes detective standing on his door step. Good evening sir, my name is Detective Haze the male said reaching his hand out to shake Billie's and this young lady is Detective Taylor We're from homicide. The female detective shook Billie's hand as well.

"We are here to speak with Nicole white." Detective Haze said as he looked passed Billie into the house Um, would she happen to be here." He asked as Billie noticed what he was doing and stepped out the house closing the door himself cutting the detectives view of his house completely off.

"What is this concerning Billie asked as he caught Detective Taylor checking his chest and arms out.

Knowing she was caught she looked into his eyes

"We didn't mean to disturb you but we need to ask her a few questions about her where about yesterday between the hours of 9:30 am to 1:30 pm Detective Taylor stated then licked her lips as she felt her panties getting wet as Billie looked her up and down. This woman is way too good looking to be a pig Billie thought as Detective cleared his throat to regain control of the conversation and get both their attention.

"Yes there was a murder at the LAX Hilton and we found her finger prints there with several other peoples, so as part of our investigation we are talking to all of these people we don't want to leave any stones unturned." Billie's mind went blank as he remembered Kelly and the things he had seen and heard on the news.

"Sir, are you okay?" Detective Taylor asked with concern in her voice. Billie snapped out his trans

"Yeah! Em, I'm fine." He stated still lost in thought.

"She isn't her right now she stepped out for a little while, but as soon as she returns, I'll be sure to tell her you stopped by. But I can a sure you that she had nothing to do with what happened there." Billie stated as everything that he heard on the news continue to play in his head.

"Oh, we are not saying she does, it our job to check all leads, be sure to give her this and have her call us." Detective Haze said handing Billie a card

"By the way, I didn't catch your name Detective Haze said as he looked over his shoulder, hearing a car pulling into the drive way, Billie Ward," Billie stated as he watched Monica park and coming walking up the drive way with concern written all over her face. All 6 Sheriff's turn around as Monica approached. Detective Taylor turned on her heels quickly facing Monica

"Ms. White?" She stated looking Monica directly into her eyes.

"No, I'm Ms. Tillis. Excuse me!" Monica said pushing her way passed the Sheriffs and both Detectives so she could stand by Billie's side. Do you have any ID Detective Haze asked with a smile. I sure do Monica stated. As she looked in her purse, grabbed her ID then handed it to him.

"Here you go!" Monica said faking a smile. Detective Haze looked it over then handed it back to her. Thank you Ms. Tills we were just leaving!" He stated still looking Monica over as she put her ID back in her purse.

"Is everything okay? Monica asked hoping this didn't have anything to do with her run in with Nicole at Wal-Mart.

"Yes everything's fine Ms. Tillis no need for concern we just need to ask Ms. White, a few questions but she isn't here, is she a friend of yours," Detective Haze asked admiring Monica beauty

"Yes she is!" Monica lied "but I haven't seen her today, I was just stopping by to talk to my boss about pay roll!" Monica said calmly. Detective Taylor looked Monica up and down the frowned "so you haven't seen or heard from her today correct? Detective Taylor asked with skepticism. Monica sensing the attitude smiled

"No, I haven't, sorry that I can't be of more help to you!" Monica stated then wrapped her arm inside of Billie's

"well if we are done I'd like to get back in my house and finish cooking dinner and now deal with my secretary and payroll" Billie said trying to get rid of the Detectives and cops.

"We'll be in touch Detective Taylor said smiling at Billie before they walked off 'you do that Monica said sarcastically as she grabbed Billie's hand and opened the door pulling him into the house as the Detectives and Sheriffs got in their cars and drove off.

"We need to talk!" Monica said as she closed the door and locked it. What's wrong Mo, and how did you know I was here Billie asked as he noticed the serious look on Monica's face. Monica took a deep breath then exhaled for the first time since the incident at Wal-Mart she relaxed

"Daddy while I was at the funeral home waiting for you to get there Nicole tried to kill me and our baby!" Nicole did what!" Billie stated in disbelief.

"When was this and why were you at the funeral home waiting for me?" He asked still trying to register what Monica just told him

"It was about an hour in a half ago maybe two hours, I texted you and told you that the funeral home had called me and wanted us to come down and finalize everything about momma's funeral. I got a text from you saying to meet you there at 4:45 but then you re texted me and told me 5: 15, so I did as you asked." Monica said showing him her phone so he could read the text messages.

"That wasn't from me!" Billie stated as he looked at the number it was sent from (which was his) and read the text

"I didn't send that Billie stated in disbelief as he realized Nicole must of unlocked his phone and sent them. Well I figured that once Nicole drove up on me trying to blow my brains out Monica said realizing how close she had come to losing her and her baby's life.

"She almost accomplished her goal but I noticed something was wrong when I got out the car to greet you, well, who I thought was and the car speeded up. N-E how

I dived back in the car, that's when the gun shots started." Monica said as she looked at Billie who was staring into outer space with his mouth open in shock.

"That's fuckin crazy!" Billie uttered still lost in thought about what Monica just said happen

"Now my turn to ask questions!" Monica stated while looking him up and down with an attitude.

"Why are you here half-dressed and what are you doing over here?" Monica asked then crossed her arms across her chest looking into his eyes waiting for her answer. Billie signed

"I came over here to talk to Nicole because she is pregnant and I wanted to be in my child's life. No matter what happened between me and her the child didn't ask to be here and is innocent he or she deserves to have both parents in their life whether their together or not!" Billie stated still having a hard time digesting what Monica just told him Monica wanted to be mad but couldn't because Billie handling his responsibilities was one of the reasons she loved him so much.

"Okay I can totally understand that and I got your back on that 100% anything that's a part of you I'll love, but nigga you still ain't explain why you walking around half dressed. Monica said then put her hands on her hips while still looking him in his eyes.

"Mo I was fixing a few things around the..." Monica put her right hand up which made Billie cut his sentence short.

"Daddy don't lie to me, I would rather be mad at you but know you told me the truth then have you sit here and lie to my face and think that it's okay, then the truth comes out later and I hate you and distrust you.

We are human I can forgive you for a mistake but if you lie to me then it wasn't a mistake you did it to hurt me because when I find out you lied to me and had the chance to come clean, that's just what's going to happen you're going to hurt me!" Monica stated then kissed him tenderly.

"No matter what, tell me the truth. But right now is not the time to discuss this, but once we get somewhere and can talk I expect you to be honest with me. Right now we need to get the fuck out this house there is a lot that is happen that I need to share with you but this house it not the place to do it!" Monica stated as she remembered what took place in the very spot she stood just a few months ago.

"You right Mo!" Billie said bringing her back to reality. Billie kissed her on the lips which made her pussy twitch.

"I'll tell you the truth I promise, now wait here!" Billie said as he ran up the stairs to get his shirt and shoes I love this nigga Monica thought to herself as she watched him coming down the stairs two at a time putting his shirt on. Once down the stairs he kissed Monica again I love you and I'm glad you're okay!" Billie said sincerely,

"Now come on, let's get out of here!" He stated as he opened the front door and stepped outside Monica gladly followed behind him looking toward the street for any Detectives or police cars as he locked the door. Once at their cars Monica stopped Billie before he got in his Jag.

"Daddy I used my phone to GPS your car that's how I found you and I sh..." Billie put his finger to Monica lips.

"Now is not the place or time he said then kissed her forehead as he noticed some of the neighbors outside being nosey.

"Follow me to the hotel and we can talk there okay baby!" Monica shook her head up and down as Billie smacked her on her but now come on let's get out of here!" Monica got in her car hoping she would be able to tell Billie everything that had happen before shit got ugly and all hell broke loose.

Billie got in his car and pulled his phone out his pocket as he pulled out his driveway and on to Alvern he put his phone on the car charger then cut it on. As he turned off Alvern and on to Centinela he paired his cell phone with his Jaguars blue tooth then read his most recent text:

Billie call me A-Sap very important please call me back emergency! Tee

Billie took a deep breath then exhaled

"What the fuck else could go wrong!" He thought to himself as he looked through his rear view mirror making sure Monica was behind him as he got on to the 405 freeway head to the LAX Hilton he look through a few more of his texts which was also from Tasha saying call her and began to feel worried about her

"Fuck!" He said out loud as he merged into to traffic knowing that Tasha wouldn't send a text like this unless something was really wrong. Billie hit a button on his steering wheel

"Please state your command!" The woman's voice said through the car speakers.

"Call Tasha!" Billie stated as he got caught in bumper to bumper traffic.

"Calling Tasha!" The woman's voice said over the car speakers then dialed the number. Billie looked through his rear view mirror to locate Monica, just as he spotted her changing lanes and getting back behind him Tasha's number began ringing throughout his car.

Billie sat back in his seat relaxing as traffic slowly moved listening to the phone ring and waiting for Tasha to answer so he could find out just what was so urgent that she had to leave him 22 voicemails and 17 text messages.

She walked toward the doctor who had been in charge of Nicole's emergency operation. Doctor Willis smiled warmly as Tasha approached.

"How are you doing, Ms. Ward?" he asked, sincerely concerned for her wellbeing.

"I'm okay. I need to see my nephew," Tasha stated, getting straight to the point.

Doctor Willis took a deep breath, then exhaled. After 20 minutes of doing all he could to save Nicole's life, he pronounced her dead and exited the emergency room. Once in the hallway, he informed Tasha of what had happened, then held her for several minutes as she went into hysteria over the loss of her sister. As he sat Tasha in a chair in front of the emergency room, Doctor Willis informed Tasha that they had been able to save her baby. However, they weren't sure if the little boy was going to make it because he was born almost four months early.

Tasha, shook up over Nicole's death, didn't react to the news about the baby at the time. Now in her right state of mind, she wanted to see her nephew, the child her sister had brought into this world before she took her last breath.

"Okay, no problem, Ms. Ward!" Doctor Willis said as he waved one of the nurses over to him. He spoke to the nurse in a very low but firm tone for a few seconds, then turned back towards Tasha.

"Nurse Bowman will take you to your nephew's room. Let me know if there is anything else. I'll be here all night!"

Tasha shook Doctor Willis' hand.

"Thank you!" Tasha stated as she followed Nurse Bowman down the hall and through a set of double doors. The nurse guided her into a dimly lit room, then smiled.

"Just hit the call button if you need anything!" Nurse Bowman said as she walked back the way she had brought them, leaving Tasha in the room alone. Tears rushed down Tasha's face as she walked over to the tiny incubator that was the temporary home of Nicole's newborn baby boy.

"He's beautiful!" Tasha stated as she reached her hand through the E-holes in the incubator and caressed her nephew's tiny little hand.

"Hey there, Little Billie Doreah Ward, Jr." Tasha said as she ran her fingers across the baby's fingertips. Her nephew reacted to her voice and stirred gently as he grabbed Tasha's finger. Once again, tears began to fall from her eyes. Tasha couldn't control or help it. As she gazed lovingly at Nicole's son, she felt overwhelmed at the thought of Nicole not being able to see her child grow up. Tasha continued rubbing Little Billie's hand.

"Auntie got you, little man!" Tasha stated as she felt all the love she had for Nicole transferring into her son.

"I swear on my life and my unborn child's that I'm going to protect you from any harm. I'll die before I let anything happen to you!" Tasha stated, meaning every word that she said and ready to lay down her life to prove it. She felt she owed Nicole that much.

Prematurely born, Little Billie weighed only four pounds and three ounces. The newborn had been traumatized twice while inside his mother's womb and was struggling for his life. The breathing tubes that were inserted inside his tiny chest cavity helped to sustain his breathing. The doctors didn't know if Little Billie would make it through this ordeal or not, but they were doing everything in their power to make sure he did.

"A miracle baby, that's what you are, and Auntie loves you and so does your daddy. You have to be strong for us!" Tasha stated while gently caressing Little Billie's head. Tasha sat with her nephew for hours, talking to him and singing all of her and Nicole's favorite songs. Tasha said a silent prayer for Nicole's soul, and for Little Billie's life to be spared. After seeing that Little Billie was sound asleep,

Tasha exited the room with tears in her eyes. Once in the hallway, she pulled her cell phone out of her purse. Just as she was about to try and reach Billie for the eighteenth time, Doctor Willis walked up to her.

"So how was the visit with our little trooper?" he asked smiling.

"It was wonderful," Tasha said, smiling for the first time since Nicole had been shot.

"He is beautiful!"

Doctor Willis nodded his head in agreement.

"Yes, he is a handsome little devil. Sure to be a heartbreaker."

Tasha laughed.

"Yeah, just like his daddy," she stated, remembering why she had her phone in her hand.

Doctor Willis cleared his throat.

"I don't mean to kill the moment, but your sister made me promise to tell you something before she died," Doctor Willis said, then paused, waiting for Tasha to give him the okay to continue.

Tasha, feeling her emotions about to overwhelm her, looked into his eyes.

"And what was that?" she asked, using all her willpower to hold back her tears and control her emotions.

"She told me to tell you she loved you, that she forgives you and to take care of her baby no matter what. She is counting on you to take care of y'all's family and to protect what's yours!"

Tasha began crying uncontrollably as she remembered Nicole's granny telling them both the last part of what the doctor had just told her before she had died fifteen years ago.

"Thank you so much!" Tasha uttered as Doctor Willis handed her a handkerchief.

Epilogue

Tasha sat in the hallway outside of Nicole's hospital room with her hands over her face mourning the loss of her best friend. Tasha uncontrollably rocked back and forward in shock, feeling overwhelmed as she thought about all the good times her and Nicole had shared throughout the years. Tasha wiped her face as she laughed, remembering her and Nicole's first day at elementary school and how Nicole had taken up for her when a little boy by the name of Terry McGee had almost knocked her down running in the hallway in front of their classroom.

"Excuse me, but I think you need to apologize to my sister for bumping into her and knocking her down!" A 5-year-old Nicole stated, looking Terry McGee straight in his eyes with her right hand on her hip while her left held her My little Pony lunch pail.

"I'm not apologizing to no stupid girl. She shouldn't have been in my way!" little Terry McGee said with an attitude, then rolled his eyes at both of them. With no hesitation, Nicole smacked him upside his head with her lunch pail, which made him fall to the ground holding his head in a daze.

"My nanny said that little boys that are bullies and hit girls are punks!" Nicole stated to little Terry McGee as she looked at him on the ground holding his head in pain. Nicole rolled her eyes and neck together at him, then grabbed Tasha's hand. As they walked into their classroom, Tasha kicked little Terry McGee in his Johnson for good measure and stuck her tongue out at him, leaving him in pain and crying like a baby. From that day forward, Tasha and Nicole handled anyone that did anything to either of them together.

"I got you, sis!" Tasha stated as she stood up, determined not to let Nicole down after all the years that she had been there for her and by her side.

"I got you, Cola !" Tasha said, as her head in her lap as thoughts of Nicole along with moments they shared filled her mind. She began crying silently as she realized she would never get to see Nicole smile, laugh or spend time with her again. Tasha started rocking back and forward, wishing Billie had answered his phone and was there to help her through this horrible ordeal. She continued crying until she drifted off to sleep next to the incubator while holding Little Billie's hand, not realizing that Billie was calling because her phone was inside her purse and she couldn't hear it ringing...

To Be Continued . . ... *Be on the lookout for*
Unfaithful 3 Tasha's Vengeance

ABOUT THE AUTHOR

Billie Dureyea Shell was born in Compton, California. He graduated from the University of Northridge with a Bachelor's Degree in Business Administration. For 12 years, he served in the United States Navy Special Operations Team, 6 years were served in Fullujah, Iraq.

He lives in Ladera Heights with his wife and children, with whom he devotes all of his free time to when he is not writing. He is a business owner who loves to give back to the community and tries to help at-risk youth. He hopes to leave a literary legacy behind for future Urban Writers.